the misadventures of

Gold Flakes for Breakfast

PAUL BUCHANAN & ROD RANDALL

CPH®
SAINT LOUIS

The Misadventures of Willie Plummet

Invasion from Planet X
Submarine Sandwiched
Anything You Can Do, I Can Do Better
Ballistic Bugs
Battle of the Bands
Gold Flakes for Breakfast

Cover illustration by John Ward.
Back cover photo by Ira Lippke.

Copyright © 1998 Rod Randall
Published by Concordia Publishing House
3558 S. Jefferson Avenue, St. Louis, MO 63118-3968

Manufactured in the United States of America

Library of Congress Cataloging-in-Publication Data

Buchanan, Paul, 1959-
    Gold flakes for breakfast / Paul Buchanan and Rod Randall.
        p.   cm. — (The misadventures of Willie Plummet)
    Summary: During a church service project, Willie launches a treasure hunt when he falls into a mysterious cellar that was once an outlaw hideout.
        ISBN 0-570-05045-6
        [1. Buried treasure—Fiction. 2. Robbers and outlaws—Fiction. 3. Christian life—Fiction.] I. Randall, Rod, 1962-   . II. Title. III. Series: Buchanan, Paul, 1959- Misadventures of Willie Plummet.
    PZ7.B87717Go 1998
    [Fic]—dc21   97-42218
                                                                                                              AC

1   2   3   4   5   6   7   8   9   10   07   06   05   04   03   02   01   00   99   98

For my parents,
Dr. and Mrs. Don Howard Randall

Contents

The Jet-powered Pogo Stick

When I went with the youth group to the Pike Estate, the last thing on my mind was buried gold. All I could think about was how to get out of the task at hand: yard work.

Colonel Pike lived in a big house near downtown Glenfield. He had white hair and skin like saddle leather. When he wasn't in church or at the five-and-dime, he was on his porch sipping Cactus Coolers and talking about the Old West. At 80 years old, the Colonel was unable to care for his property all alone and he couldn't afford to hire a gardener. The massive grounds were totally overgrown.

That's when my church youth group got involved. Our youth pastor suggested that we fix the place up for free as a service project. And since I'm in the youth group …

"Felix, we'll never get this done at the rate you're going," I told him, hoping he would get the lead out. "My Great-grandma Plummet can dig faster than you."

"In that case, Willie, maybe you should try helping," Felix said, pausing to wipe the sweat from his face.

"If I help, who's going to supervise you?" I reasoned.

Felix and I were in the corner of the backyard. Our job was to dig a hole for an ornamental tree. Colonel Pike wanted to have his house registered as a national historic landmark. He hoped that some attractive landscaping would help with the approval process.

"This ground is rock hard," Felix complained. He jumped on the shovel and bounced back higher than he had jumped.

"Here, try this," I said, handing Felix a pick.

He grabbed the handle, but the iron head dropped straight to the ground. "This thing weighs a ton," he complained.

"That's the idea," I told him. "The heavier the pick, the better it digs."

Straining with all his might, Felix hoisted the pick to his shoulder. He stumbled backward and forward, trying to keep his balance. The pick handle was thicker than Felix's arms. I feared the iron head would snap his frame in two.

"Whoa!" he cried.

I tried to encourage him. "Use your legs, not your back. Just lift and swing."

Felix looked worried. Sweat dripped from the end of his nose. He gave me a nod and lifted the pick over his head, but he didn't bring it down. He didn't have enough momentum.

"Uh-oh," he said. He balanced the pick high above his head. For a moment he looked like the leaning tower of Pisa. Then he leaned a little too far—straight at me. "Look out!" he shouted. I lunged out of the way just in time. Felix landed hard, sinking the pick deep into the soil.

"Way to go, Ace," I said. "You've got to be more careful."

Felix just stared at the sky, still holding the pick handle. "Don't worry, Willie. I didn't get hurt," he said.

"But *I* almost did," I told him. "You could have killed me with that thing. There's got to be an easier way to get this job done."

"Maybe I can help," a man said, walking toward us. He introduced himself as Jake, the foreman of a road crew that was working down the street. Jake had thick forearms and calloused hands. He wore a green John Deere hat that was faded from the sun. Apparently he had been watching us. "I know what a bear this hard soil can be. Would you like to borrow our jackhammer?"

"I like the sound of that," I said. With that, Jake walked away to get the power tool.

"I don't," Felix countered. "Aren't those things dangerous?"

"How dangerous can it be if that guy is offering it to us?" I asked. "But if it makes you feel any better, this time you can supervise me."

When Jake returned with the jackhammer, he gave us a brief demonstration of how it worked, then handed it to me. Some of the kids from the youth group gathered around, which made me feel really cool. I placed the jackhammer chisel against the ground.

"Here goes nothing," I said, flipping the power switch to "on." *Chunk-a-chunk-a-chunk-a!* The jackhammer rattled me from head to toe. The chisel chipped and plunged, breaking through the hard dirt.

"Y-y-yes!" I yelled through chattering teeth. More kids gathered around, gasping in amazement.

"Turn it off, Willie!" Felix shouted. He sliced a finger across his throat. "Cut! Cut!"

I hit the power switch as fast as I could. "Why? What's wrong?"

"My turn," he said, taking hold of the jackhammer.

I hesitated, not sure if Felix could handle it. "Are you sure about this?"

"Positive," he said, pushing me away.

I didn't know what to say. Neither did the rest of the youth group. They just stared in anticipation, looking as uneasy as I felt. Normally Felix wouldn't have tried the pick, let alone the jackhammer. But today he wouldn't let up. It was as though he had something to prove.

Oh, well, I thought, *it's not that hard to control.* So what if he gets a little shook up. How bad could it be? As soon as Felix turned it on, I found out.

"Yikes!" he hollered.

The jackhammer took off like a jet-powered pogo stick! Felix was hanging on for dear life. His feet caught more air than Michael Jordan's. The jackhammer, and Felix, crossed the lawn, the flower bed, and even the back porch, before turning around.

"W-W-Willie!" Felix cried. "L-L-Look out!" The jackhammer came right for me, as if on a mission to destroy. Felix fluttered behind the handlebars.

"Run for your lives!" I shouted.

Chunk-a-chunk-a-chunk-a! The jackhammer pounded on, out of control. Youth group members flew in all directions, diving for cover.

I would have too, but I tripped. "No!" I screamed as the jackhammer bore down.

"M-M-Move, W-W-Willie," Felix called out. There was no time to move. I lunged and grabbed the jackhammer. It whipped me through the air as if I were a flag. Felix let go, then scrambled to get out of the way. But I was bouncing right toward him …

Chunk-a-chunk-a- Stop. The jackhammer went silent.

Jake stood a few feet away, holding the unplugged cord in his hand. "Maybe this wasn't such a good idea after all," he said, glaring at us. Walking over, he picked up the jackhammer and returned to his road crew. A guy with a white shirt and tie chewed him out when he got there.

"Bummer for Jake," I said, thinking that guy in the tie had to be Jake's boss. Looking around, I surveyed the damage. "And bummer for the Pike Estate. Forget the historic landmark designation. This place looks more like a national disaster area."

After giving Felix a big dose of angry looks, our fellow youth group members returned to their projects to undo what Felix had done. I grabbed a shovel and dug out the loose dirt broken up by the jackhammer. But that didn't last long. Soon I was down to hard ground once again.

Felix remained where he fell, sulking. "Who knew it was so hard to steer a jackhammer?" he asked. "Of course, if my biceps were bigger, it would have been a breeze." He threw a pebble at a large bottlebrush plant covered with red flowers. With its dense leaves and droopy branches, it looked more like a hut than an overgrown bush. The bush responded with a *yelp*.

"What was that?" I asked. With a wag of her tail, Sadie, my black-and-white cocker spaniel, crawled from beneath the bush's thick branches. Strands of red bottlebrush clung to her fur. She headed straight for Felix and licked his face.

"Sadie, what are you doing here?" I moaned. "If Mom knows you got out, we're both history."

But Felix was glad to see her. "Thanks, Sadie," he said. "At least you don't think I'm a jerk."

"Neither do I," I told him. "Now get over here and start digging."

I was about to start digging again when another idea came to mind. It was even better than the jackhammer. Sadie. Her digging skills would make a bulldozer proud. Mom's demolished rosebushes proved it.

"Come here, Sadie," I said, pointing at the hole. "Dig, girl. Dig." Sadie didn't budge. She just looked at me sideways, like I was nuts.

"Right here," I said, dropping to my knees. I scraped the dirt with my fingernails. "Dig, Sadie. You can do it. Just pretend it's Mom's flower bed." Sadie didn't move. She glanced up at Felix, then back at me. I didn't give up.

"Felix, get over here. If we both show her how much fun it is, she's bound to dig."

Felix shook his head. "Shouldn't you and I just work harder and do it ourselves?"

"Yeah, sure," I laughed. "That's a good one. But seriously, come here and help me entice Sadie."

"Forget it," he said. "I've embarrassed myself enough already."

"No one is watching," I told him. "Now, hurry, Sadie needs some motivation." Reluctantly Felix joined me in digging like a dog. Scratching at the ground, we flung the dirt between our legs.

"It's working," I said. "She's coming over. Quick! Howl and bark like we're having fun—and wag your tail."

"Woof! Woof!" Felix let out.

"Oww-woo," I howled, shaking my behind. Sadie sat next to us and stared.

"More," I demanded.

"Woof! Woof! Woof! Oww-woo," Felix continued. But just as Sadie began to dig, she stopped and looked past us. Her ears pricked up and she cocked her head in keen interest.

Looking up, I knew why. The entire youth group had gathered around us. Even Colonel Pike was there. My face burned bright red. Felix tried to hide in our three-inch hole, but it didn't work. After a moment of awkward silence, the group burst into a chorus of laughter. Kids doubled over, holding their sides. Others wiped away tears. Colonel Pike was laughing too.

Then the wisecracks rang out.

"Sit, Willie. Sit."

"Fetch the stick, Felix."

"Roll over, Willie."

"Heel, Felix!" Frozen with embarrassment, we didn't respond. That only made things worse.

"Bad dog!"

"No more drinking out of the toilet for you."

At that I wished I were a dog, as in an attack dog. Then I could snarl, bare my teeth, and scare everyone away. But all Felix and I could do was wait it out. Eventually the kids returned to their projects and we did the same. Felix's suggestion turned out to be our only option. We worked harder. Eventually we got the hole dug and the ornamental tree planted.

When everything was done, we gathered on the porch with Colonel Pike. He told us that his grandfather, Judge Donald Pike, known to everyone as J.D., had bought the property from the legendary Pistol Pete. "In his prime there wasn't a man alive faster with a six-shooter than Pistol Pete," Colonel Pike told us. "But even the fastest gun ain't enough when you're outgunned 20 to one. Pete died on this very front porch when the Crawly Gang surrounded him."

I was about to ask why the Crawly Gang surrounded Pistol Pete when the photographer from the *Glenfield Gazette* arrived to take pictures. Colonel Pike immediately left to show the place off, and I didn't blame him. With the neatly trimmed lawn and freshly planted flowers, the Pike Estate looked beautiful.

Before we left, we returned to the front porch with Colonel Pike to pose for a picture. The tough part was getting Sadie to sit next to me. She kept returning to that bottlebrush plant like a pirate goes after treasure. I wanted to ask more about Pistol Pete but, thanks to my dog, I had to forget about it.

"Knock it off, Sadie," I scolded her. Grabbing her collar, I yanked her back to the porch. But Sadie's eyes were on that hut-like bush every step of the way. It wasn't until later that night that I found out why.

Two Desperados

My parents just shook their heads when I explained what had happened at the Pike Estate. Orville and Amanda, my older siblings, were equally amazed. We were sitting at the patio table finishing a dinner of barbecued ribs. Sadie sat beneath the table, gnawing on a bone.

"I'm sorry to interrupt," Mom said, "but I really don't like the dog eating here."

"But Mom," I countered, "if Sadie doesn't learn to eat *near* the table, how do you expect her to eat *at* the table with us?"

"At the table?" Mom choked out the question.

Orville jumped right in. "Yeah, Mom. Sadie can have her own place setting, right next to you."

"Stop the teasing," Mom said. "Just thinking about it makes me sick. That dog is spoiled enough as it is."

"Mom, whisper, please," I said. "You'll hurt Sadie's feelings."

"I'll hurt more than that if she doesn't shape up. You saw what she did to my roses."

As if understanding every word, Sadie quickly picked up her bone and headed to the back fence.

"Speaking of your roses, Mom," I said. "Because of them, I looked like the biggest knucklebrain in our youth group today."

"Willie, what are you talking about? You mean the jackhammer disaster wasn't the worst of it?" Amanda asked.

"I wish. When I saw Sadie, I remembered Mom's rosebushes. That's when I decided to make Sadie my secret hole-digging weapon."

"Makes sense," Dad agreed.

I nodded. "That's what I thought. But Sadie wouldn't dig. In desperation Felix and I scratched the dirt like dogs. We even howled and barked, thinking Sadie would catch a clue. But she didn't. She just looked at us like we were a couple of nuts."

"I wonder why?" Amanda asked, winking at Orville.

"The worst part was when we stopped," I explained. "The entire youth group had gathered around. I've never heard my friends laugh so loud. And you should have seen Colonel Pike. If he would have laughed any harder, he would have spit out his false teeth."

"At least Felix would have had something to dig with," Orville said.

"That's a scary thought," I added, shaking my head.

"Why? Because Colonel Pike would have gotten so mad?" Orville asked.

"No. Because Felix would have gotten bit," I explained. "You should have seen the size of those choppers."

"Enough, Willie," Dad warned. "That sounds pretty disrespectful to me."

"But Orville said stuff too," I argued.

"I know. But you started it. I don't like where this is going, and I don't want it to get any worse. Besides it's Colonel Pike's age that makes him an expert on Glenfield history. His grandfather was one of the early settlers who founded Glenfield back in the late 1800s."

"That's what the Colonel told us," I said. "He even brought up Pistol Pete and the Crawly Gang. It was totally cool. Normally when an old geezer like Colonel Pike talks history, it's about how they didn't have CD players or computers or any of the modern stuff we have. Then they brag about walking 10 miles to school with bare feet, in the snow, and uphill both ways—like that's possible."

"Willie, that's the kind of disrespect I'm talking about," Dad told me, getting mad. "If I hear you describe a senior adult as an 'old geezer' again, you're grounded."

At that I asked to be excused before my dad's warning turned into a full-blown lecture. Ever since I'd entered junior high, my dad was constantly accusing me of being disrespectful to adults, especially to him and Mom. He quoted the Fourth Commandment—"Honor your father and your mother"—all the time. If that didn't do it, he'd throw in that proverb about heeding your parents' advice. For the most part I did honor them, but sometimes they seemed out of touch with what it's like to be in junior high.

Making my way to the back fence, I looked for Sadie. With Mom on Sadie's back and Dad on mine, Sadie and I shared a common bond. We were a couple of desperados on the run from the law.

"Sadie!" I called. "Here, girl."

I listened for the jingling of the tags on her collar, expecting her to come running from behind a tree. But she didn't. "Sadie?" I shouted again.

I called her a few more times, then returned to the patio. "Mom, I can't find Sadie. Did she sneak past here?"

"No. She must have gotten out again. You'd better find her before she digs up someone else's roses," Mom warned me. "And just so you know, you have one week to get that dog under control. Otherwise, it's obedience school."

"Anything but that," I moaned. Obedience school met every Saturday at 8 A.M. Getting up for school during the week was bad enough. I couldn't imagine waking up early on Saturday too. The class lasted 10 weeks, if you passed; otherwise you had to repeat. Not only would Sadie, the outlaw, be forced into submission, I'd be a sleep-deprived zombie.

"One week," Mom threatened as I headed for the gate.

My Dad caught me on the way out. "Willie, don't you think you should take a flashlight?"

"Dad, the streetlights are on," I replied, desperate to leave the house.

"Streetlights aren't everywhere," he reminded me.

"But the full moon is," I told him, "in case you haven't noticed."

"I don't like your attitude," Dad said. "One more crack like that and Sadie won't be the only one we send to obedience school." I closed my mouth and walked through the gate, determined to leave before something else went wrong.

Tunnel Time

My search for Sadie took me next door to Phoebe's house first. Phoebe was in fourth grade and she had a major crush on me. Phoebe also had a cat named Prissy. Sometimes Sadie would stop in at Phoebe's to finish off the food that Prissy left behind.

"Sorry, Willie," Phoebe said when I explained things. "Sadie hasn't been here at all. But I'll help you look for her if you want."

"That's okay," I said. "I need to go it alone."

"What do you mean, *go it alone?*" Phoebe asked.

"That's outlaw talk. You wouldn't understand."

Phoebe just gave me a look. "Whatever."

Leaving Phoebe standing on the front step, I meandered down the street, checking neighborhood yards as I walked. Then I noticed an open side gate at the house on the corner. I heard barking that sounded like Sadie. It was coming from the backyard. Then it stopped.

"Bingo," I said, cutting across the front lawn. I walked through the open gate and along the side of the house. The barking started again, but it came from inside the house this time. *Why would Sadie be inside?* I wondered. Moving to the window, I cupped my hands and looked through the glass. Big mistake.

"AAAHHH!" a woman screamed. "A prowler! Call the police!"

"Where?" a man growled. "I'll get my 12-gauge." I heard boots stomping across the wood floor.

"I'm just looking for my dog," I mumbled in defense, stumbling backward.

The woman kept screaming so I took off. Maybe the police would believe my side of the story, maybe they wouldn't. I wasn't going to stick around long enough to find out. I sprinted down the street, breathing hard. My heart pounded like a jackhammer. Now I really was an outlaw, and I didn't like it one bit.

At the sound of sirens I ducked down an alley and cut through the park. Pausing behind a giant elm tree, I tried to figure out where Sadie could be. Then I remembered the episode at Colonel Pike's earlier in the day. Sadie kept returning to that red bottlebrush plant. Of course!

I took off again, doing my best to stay out of sight. Whenever a car drove by, I ducked, just in case it was the police. Talk about a challenge, I had to find Sadie before the police found me.

The Pike Estate was totally dark. Three stories full of windows, but not a light was on. A heavy darkness wrapped around the porch. At night the place looked kind of creepy. Good thing the moon was full.

After hopping the fence on the side of the yard, I jogged to the massive old bush. "Sadie?" I whispered. I listened for the jingling of the tags on her collar, hoping she would emerge from the dense branches. She didn't.

"Sadie?" I called softly. Dropping to my knees, I crawled under the bush. The moonlight barely filtered through the thick leaves. The soil was cool and loose—and freshly dug. It even smelled like Sadie. Pushing aside the branches, I felt my way deeper into the foliage.

"Sadie? Sa ..." My body dropped into a hole! "Help!" I yelled, sliding face first. I clawed at the dirt, trying to stop myself. It was no use. I kept falling. Plunging. Covering my head, I prayed for God's help. A moment later I hit the soft bottom of the hole with a *thud*.

It was pitch black. I was in some kind of tunnel. Feeling all around, I realized that I could stand up. *Cool*, I thought. If only I had a flashlight. Chalk one up for Dad. This time he was right.

"Sadie, I'm impressed," I said, hoping she would come jingling up. "This is some find." I took a few steps forward, feeling the darkness as I went. Then it occurred to me that there might be another hole like the one I had just dropped into. Maybe next time the landing wouldn't be so soft. Edging backward, I found the small opening that I had just fell through.

"Sadie?" I called one last time. I listened to the silence, waiting.

What's that? I wondered. A sound came from deep inside the tunnel. It wasn't Sadie's collar. It sounded more like the low growl of a grizzly bear.

I climbed into the opening and crawled as fast as I could toward the bottlebrush plant. The loose dirt gave way, but I didn't give up. I dug my feet into the damp soil. I clawed at the ground with my fingernails. The growl grew louder and closer. Tromping feet echoed through the tunnel.

I kept crawling. Moonlight glimmered through the branches. I was almost to the top.

"GRRR!" the beast closed in. I grabbed a branch of the bottlebrush plant and pulled myself out of the hole. The beast growled right behind me like it would grab my ankle and pull me back into the tunnel. Scrambling on my hands and feet, I broke free from the bottlebrush plant and crawled into the yard.

Before I could stand, the beast burst from the bush. It was a giant black dog the size of a wolf. Its dripping white teeth gleamed in the moonlight. I covered my head and envisioned the headlines in the *Glenfield Gazette:* "Willie Plummet the Prowler Gets Woofed-Down by Giant Woof-Dog."

Then a different bark caught my attention. I recognized the sound and opened my eyes. Sadie launched from the bottlebrush plant like a rocket. She lunged between me and the giant black dog. Sadie snarled in its direction. That was all it took—the other dog stopped instantly. Sadie trotted over to me and licked my face. The other dog quit growling. He wagged his tail, walked over, and licked my face too. Between him and Sadie, I felt like I was in a car wash.

Standing up, I searched around the area. There was no sign of the black dog's owner. The dog's collar read "Java" and gave a street address. I looked at my watch. It was getting late. If we hurried, I could drop Java off on my way home, assuming the police didn't pick us up first.

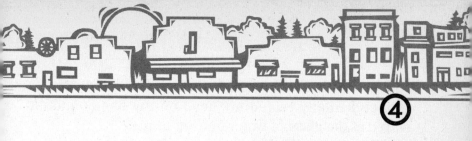

I.V. Man to the Rescue

The next day at church, I told Sam and Felix about the tunnel. Sam was totally interested, which I had expected. She is the most adventuresome girl I've ever known.

Felix, on the other hand, was still sulking over the jackhammer incident. "I'm tired of being skinny," he complained. "It's time I did something about it."

We didn't know what Felix had in mind, but we agreed to meet him in the lab after church. The lab is actually the back room of Plummet's Hobbies, my family's store. The three of us meet there when we need to formulate a plan, do an experiment, or create an invention.

Sam and I arrived on time, but Felix was nowhere in sight. While waiting for him, we discussed our plan for returning to the tunnel. Sam couldn't wait to see it, but we couldn't go until Felix arrived. So we waited. And waited.

"Where is he?" I grumbled, eager to explore the tunnel. I finally rested my head on my hands and stared at the glass of water in front of me.

Then a strange thing happened. Ripples began to form across the surface of the water.

"What's that?" I asked, sitting up.

Sam studied the glass. "Maybe you bumped the table."

"No, I didn't," I said, sitting perfectly still. The vibrations continued and grew stronger. I thought of that scene from *Jurassic Park* when the *Tyrannosaurus rex* approached the kids in the jeep.

"Maybe it's a road crew," Sam suggested. "You said one was working near the Pike Estate."

"I don't think so," I replied, looking around. Jars of model paint rattled on the shelves.

"What is it?" Sam asked, getting nervous.

Boom! Boom! The sound of footsteps, as heavy as thunder, approached the back door. Sam and I just stared, too petrified to move. The doorknob slowly turned and swung open. Our chins dropped. We couldn't believe our eyes.

"Felix? Is that you?" Sam asked, astounded.

"W-W-What happened?" I asked, shaking my head.

Boom! Boom! Felix entered the lab, rocking back and forth with the force of a *T-rex*. He wore an orange flight suit covered with what looked like a ton of iron weights.

"Felix, hold still before you shake everything off the shelves," I told him.

Felix stopped and slowly raised his hands to his hips. "Just call me I.V. Man."

"I.V. Man?" Sam asked, raising her eyebrows.

"Yep. That's short for Iron Velcro Man." Felix grabbed one of the iron plates and ripped it off his chest, then stuck it back in the same spot. "My flight suit and weights are completely covered with Velcro. All I have to do is attach the weights to the muscle area that needs developing."

"But you have weights everywhere," Sam pointed out.

"Yeah, thanks for reminding me," Felix said, looking down.

Sam and I stood up and moved around him, stunned at what we saw. Even Felix's ball cap was covered with Velcro and weights.

"I think it's a great idea, I.V. Man," I said, trying to encourage him. "After a few days in that suit, you'll have the strongest Velcro on the planet."

"Thanks, Willie," Felix replied. "That makes me feel way better."

"Then why are you still looking down?" I asked.

"I can't lift my head, that's why," Felix said.

Sam and I each grabbed an ear and lifted Felix's head.

"Ouch!" he yelled. We pulled until his head was in an upright position.

"There you go, Felix," Sam said. "Now your ears will be as big as your muscles."

"Thanks, earthling," Felix replied. "And by the way, did you call me *Felix?* I thought I told you to call me *I.V. Man.*"

Sam was quick to apologize. "Sorry, I.V. Man." I just shook my head and smiled, thankful that for once the crazy invention didn't belong to me. Rather than sit Felix down and risk never getting him to his feet again, we headed straight for the Pike Estate. This time I brought a flashlight.

The Hidden Door

With Felix under a ton of weight, the walk to Colonel Pike's was slow going. Felix rocked from side to side, pounding the pavement like an elephant. Pretty soon Sam and I were rocking with him.

"How stupid does this look?" I complained, trying to walk normally. I feared that any minute Leonard "Crusher" Grubb would show up and make us look worse than we already did. What a relief to arrive at the Pike Estate. Crossing the front porch, I knocked on the front door.

"Colonel Pike?" I called out, peering through the window of the front door. I rang the bell, then knocked again, but no one answered.

"His car's here," Sam said, pointing to a '55 Chevy at the end of the long driveway.

"Maybe he's around back," Felix suggested from the yard. He was sinking deeper by the minute. We wouldn't let him on the porch for fear he'd fall back-

ward and smash straight through the old boards as if they were toothpicks.

"It's worth a try," I agreed. We teetered around back, calling for the Colonel along the way. He still didn't appear.

"Now what?" Sam asked.

"I can at least show you the tunnel," I said. "But unless Colonel Pike gives us the okay, we shouldn't go inside."

"Sounds good to me," Sam said.

"I'm game," Felix said through clenched teeth. With all those weights pushing down on his head, he could barely move his mouth.

"Aren't you in pain?" Sam asked him. "You look miserable."

"Only when I breathe," he whispered.

"Oh, that's nice," I said. "Maybe I should pull off some of those weights."

But Felix carefully shook his head. "No pain, no gain."

At the bush I pointed beneath the branches. "The hole's in there. You'll have to squat down to see it."

Sam dropped to her knees. "Cool! There really is a hole in there. And it looks deep."

"You got that right," I said. "Can you see it, Felix?"

"You mean *I.V. Man*," he responded. "No, I can't see it."

Felix tried to kneel down to get a better look, but his strength finally gave out. He took a few steps into the red bottlebrush plant, then fell forward. I tried to stop him but couldn't. He snapped through the thick branches like they were twigs and landed face first in the hole.

"Help me!" Felix yelled, plunging straight down. We heard the heavy *thud* of his body landing on the tunnel floor.

Turning on my flashlight, I dove into the tunnel. I had to rescue Felix before the weights crushed I.V. Man like a straw puppet. I fell fast and hard.

Whack! My flashlight smashed into one of the weights. At least that's what I thought.

"Ouch!" Felix wailed, lying spread-eagle on the tunnel floor. "You just smacked me in the head with your flashlight."

"Don't worry about my light, I.V. Man. It's fine. The main thing is, I'm here to help you."

"Help me? You almost killed me," Felix complained. Just then Sam slid down the hole and kicked *me* upside the head.

"Ouch! Watch where you're going," I grumbled at her.

"No, you watch where you're going," Felix told me, still lying on his stomach.

"Why don't you both watch where you're going?" I asked, getting mad. "Otherwise you can get out of *my* tunnel."

Before Felix and Sam could respond, an angry voice echoed from deep inside the tunnel. "Your tunnel?" the voice boomed. "Who says this is *your* tunnel?"

I shined my light down the corridor. Wood beams as thick as railroad ties lined the walls every few yards. Thick wood rafters rested on top of the beams, supporting the ceiling. Was someone hiding behind one of the beams, waiting to pounce? I couldn't tell. At 20 feet from us, the tunnel turned sharply to the right.

"This is *my* tunnel!" the voice thundered from around the corner. Clanging chains filled the space between us, followed by the heavy thud of boots moving in our direction.

"You win," I shouted. "It's your tunnel." I handed Sam the flashlight. Grabbing Felix's arm, I tried to pull him up, but he weighed too much. "Come on, I.V. Man, at least help a little."

"I've fallen and I can't get up," Felix moaned.

Sam took Felix by the other arm and helped me lift him to the mouth of the hole. "Now start crawling," I explained, showing him how I'd done it yesterday. Felix crawled and scratched the dirt. He moved higher.

"You're getting there," I said. "Hurry!"

Felix lumbered ahead, halfway to freedom.

The chains clanged. The footsteps moved closer. Sam kept the flashlight on, ready to blind anyone who appeared. She never got the chance.

"Look out below!" Felix yelled as he slid back down the hole. We didn't react in time. *Whammo!* Felix landed on me and Sam like a ton of bricks. I felt like a bowling pin picked up for the spare. The flashlight flew from Sam's hand and went out.

"Way to go, I.V. Man," I complained. "You just turned the lab triangle into The Three Stooges."

The chains bore down, clanging. Without a flashlight, we couldn't see what was coming. The heavy boots closed in. If Felix didn't get off of me soon, I'd be dead before the tunnel terror had a chance to destroy me. I closed my eyes, not wanting to see my doom at hand. I expected more orders and chains.

But they never came. Instead, I heard a man chuckle. When I opened my eyes, I couldn't believe what I saw.

Colonel Pike stood over us with a lantern in his hand. He grinned from ear to ear. "I always did like The Three Stooges," he told us.

"Me too," I said, gasping for air. "Felix, get off of us!" Sam's silence concerned me. I feared she already had suffocated.

"I can't move," Felix said.

"Let me help," Colonel Pike offered. He pulled off some of the Velcro weights and helped Felix to his feet.

I stared at Sam, fearing the worst. After a few deep breaths, she sat up.

"Sorry if I scared you kids," Colonel Pike continued. "I didn't know who you were. I see now that you boys are from the church group that was here yesterday."

"That's us all right," I said. "Sorry about coming down here without your permission. Felix sort of fell into the hole that my dog, Sadie, dug."

"Your dog, Sadie, huh?"

I nodded. "She may have had some help, but I'm sure she was the brains behind the operation. You should see what she does to my mom's rosebushes."

Colonel Pike shook his head in amazement. "Of all the dogs that have crossed through my yard, not a one has ever sniffed out this tunnel."

"Sadie's a digger, that's for sure," I said. With the help of Colonel Pike, I found my flashlight and turned it on. "So what's this tunnel for?"

"Only Pistol Pete can answer that question. Since he died more than 100 years ago, we may never know," Colonel Pike explained. "According to my grandfather, J.D. Pike, Pete first dug this tunnel in search of gold. Later he kept it as a secret getaway."

"A getaway from whom?" Sam asked.

"Indians, gunslingers, bandits, you name it," the Colonel told us. "Pete didn't trust anyone, except, of course, his dog, Sandy. She was loyal to the end."

I glanced around, unable to contain my excitement. "This is so cool! Do you think Pete used this tunnel in his gunfight against the Crawly Gang?"

"He could have," Colonel Pike replied.

"If that's the case, why did Pistol Pete die on the porch?" Felix asked. "And why did the Crawly Gang come after Pistol Pete anyway? Were they out to settle some old score?"

"I wish I had an answer for all your questions," Colonel Pike said. "But I don't. And neither did my daddy, nor his daddy before him."

"Do you know how Pistol Pete and J.D. became friends?" I asked.

"That I do know," Colonel Pike replied. "Pete was on trial for claim jumping. A miner accused Pete of stealing his gold. Pete said it was a case of mistaken identity. J.D. sided with Pete, even though a lot of folks thought Pete was guilty. To show his gratitude, Pete caught the real claim jumper himself. After that, Pistol Pete and J.D. became friends."

I used my flashlight to search the length of the tunnel. It was about six feet high and five feet wide. Beams lined the sides and ceiling to prevent a cave-in. It definitely looked more like an old gold mine than a getaway tunnel.

Colonel Pike turned his attention to Felix. "Partner, I'm still trying to figure out what in blazes you're doing in that orange suit."

I shined my light on Felix. For the first time, I noticed how funny he looked. The red bottlebrush strands clung to the Velcro like thick hair.

"I'm I.V. Man. It stands for Iron Velcro," Felix said. "I'm trying to build up my muscles by lifting these weights."

"Your muscles look plenty big to me," Colonel Pike replied. "And I'm no expert on weight lifting, but I think you're supposed to take a break between sets. How long you been hauling those weights around?"

"About two hours," Felix said.

"Well, cowboy, I'd say you're due for a break." Colonel Pike pulled off some more of the weights and handed them to me and Sam. "Now, who's ready for a tunnel tour?"

"Me!" we shouted in unison.

"Then giddyap," Colonel Pike said. "Let's go." Colonel Pike strutted through the tunnel, and we followed behind. The spurs on his boots jingled with each step.

"That explains the chain sound," I said. "What's with the spurs?"

"A friend of mine has an ornery horse that needs training," he said.

"You still ride horses?" I asked with a gasp. "Aren't you a little ..."

"Old?" the Colonel finished, reading my mind.

I fumbled over my words. "Well, it's just that ... you are kind of ... what I mean is ..."

"Don't you worry about me none. That horse may be younger and stronger than I am, but when it comes to smarts, he's got a lot to learn." The Colonel gave us a wink and led us through the tunnel. As we walked, I noticed a passageway that veered to the left.

"Where does that go?" I asked.

"It dead ends a little ways down," Colonel Pike replied. "I couldn't tell you why it's there."

"Maybe Pistol Pete used it for an alternate escape route," Sam suggested.

"Could have," Colonel Pike admitted. "But at the end of that detour, it's solid rock."

"Just like my muscles," Felix said, getting a second wind. He puffed out his chest as he walked.

The tunnel turned to the right again. I tried to imagine what we were under. The air smelled stuffy and old. Lots of small holes dotted the walls of the tunnel. Suddenly Colonel Pike stopped and shined his light on one of the wall beams. "Have a look here," he said, pointing at words etched into the wood. It read:

PISTOL PETE
SANDY
1881

SOLD TO
JD PIKE
1886

"J.D. Pike was your grandfather, right Colonel?" Felix asked.

"He sure was. He bought this property from Pistol Pete back when Glenfield, as you know it, didn't exist. There was nothing but a dry goods store, a bank, and a few other buildings. Even the big house above us was nothing but a little one-room ranch house."

"What do you mean by *above us?*" I asked. "We've walked a long way from where we started. We're probably under the bank or library by now."

"It's easy to lose your sense of direction in a tunnel. I think that's why Pistol Pete liked it so much. Look here." Colonel Pike pushed on the beam with the names carved into it until it swung to the side. "That's a mighty narrow door, but you'd never find it either."

Turning sideways, Colonel Pike squeezed through the beam-wide door, and we followed. Pushing aside a buffalo hide that hung from the wall, we entered a damp cellar. From there we headed upstairs to the living room of the Pike Estate.

"How about a round of Cactus Coolers?" Colonel Pike asked.

"Sure," I said, eager to learn more about the Old West and Pistol Pete.

Colonel Pike disappeared into the kitchen. He came back moments later carrying a tray with four glasses of a pink concoction. We each took a glass. The drinks were ice cold and delicious.

Felix, Sam, and I followed Colonel Pike out to the back porch, ready to ask the Colonel more questions. We never got the chance.

A man stepped around the side of the house and walked up the stairs to the porch. He had on work boots and jeans with a neatly pressed white shirt and a tie.

"If it isn't the transportation supervisor himself," Colonel Pike snapped. "What do you want, Rennis?"

"This is for you," he said, attempting to hand the Colonel an envelope.

"If it's what I think it is, you can keep it. As far as I'm concerned, it ain't worth the paper it's printed on," the Colonel told the man.

"It's official now, whether you read it or not," Rennis replied. When Colonel Pike wouldn't accept the envelope, Rennis placed it on the porch bannister. "You have until four o'clock this Friday, Colonel. Then I'll be back with my crew." Rennis offered us a forced grin, then headed back around the side of the house.

I was dying to know what was in the envelope, but before I could ask, the Colonel grabbed it and stood up. "Well, partners, I'm afraid I've got things that need tending to. I'm going to have to ask you to leave. Oh, and by the way ..." he paused to make eye contact with each one of us, "other than me, there's not a person alive on this earth that's been in Pistol Pete's tunnel. If you can keep it under your hat, I'd be much obliged."

"In Felix's case that will be easy," Sam said. "His hat weighs 10 pounds."

"Adios," Colonel Pike said.

When he went inside, we stood there on the porch, staring at one another, still so stunned by the day's events that we couldn't bring ourselves to leave.

Casserole Paws

On Monday I was still stewing over the envelope that Mr. Rennis brought Colonel Pike. Sam, who had come home with me after school, was with me in the den, just as curious. We wondered if a problem had come up regarding the national historic landmark approval.

The tunnel was also on my mind. I really wanted to see it again and have a look around. The hard part was knowing how to approach the Colonel. And with all the racket coming from the kitchen, it was hard to come up with a plan. Sadie kept getting in the way as my mom tried to make dinner.

"Sadie, get down! Now!" Mom shouted.

"Boy, your mom sure gets after that dog," Sam pointed out.

"Better Sadie than me," I said, thankful to be in the den.

"I never thought of it like that," Sam said.

"Take it from a pro," I told her. "If you want to look like a saint, get yourself a bad dog. The more trouble the dog gets into, the better you look."

Sam raised her eyebrows. "So that's why you won't take Sadie to obedience school."

"That and I don't want to get up on Saturday morning," I confessed.

"Get off me!" Mom ordered, her voice full of rage. "Willie! Get in here right now!"

"So much for the safety of the den," I moaned. Sam followed me into the kitchen.

"Look what your dog did," Mom stated. She pointed at her shirt.

I tried to make the best of what I saw. "That's a nice pattern. It really looks cute on you."

"Cute? Willie, these are paw prints made from casserole. Think about it," Mom fumed.

"Casserole?" I said with wonder. "Are you sure? I thought that was part of the design."

Sadie wagged her tail and looked up at my mom as if she had just done her a favor. Mom pushed Sadie away and turned to me. "Willie, I'm not in the mood for your excuses."

"Sorry, Mom. I'm just trying to make the best of the situation," I explained. "Sadie doesn't mean any harm."

Mom cleaned her blouse with a wet paper towel. "I realize that. In some cases she just doesn't know

any better. Which is why you need to take her to obedience school."

I was about to come up with an excuse why that
wasn't necessary, but Sadie didn't give me a chance.
She stood up on her hind legs and returned her paws
to the casserole dish.

"Sadie!" Mom shouted.

Sadie dropped down and took off for the living
room, tracking casserole across the carpet. I wanted
to take off with her because I knew I would catch an
earful. Instead of running, though, I tried to calm my
mom's anger.

"Sadie's paws are semi-clean. Besides a little dirt
won't hurt. Isn't that where we get our vitamins and
minerals?" I looked to Sam for support.

Sam shrugged. "Sure, I guess there are some ..."

"There you have it," I said. "Now that casserole is
fortified."

"Does that mean you're ready to try some?" Mom
asked.

"Actually, I had my vitamins at breakfast," I said,
trying to be diplomatic. "Sorry."

"That's just what I thought," Mom said. "Now
clean up that dog and take her outside. You've got one
hour to teach her some manners or she'll stay outside
until she learns some."

"But she gets lonely outside," I reasoned. "And
she already obeys. It just depends on the command."

I turned and shouted into the living room. "Sadie! Do *not* come here."

When Sadie didn't return, a sheepish grin spread across my face. "See, Mom. How's that for obedience?"

"What kind of command is, 'Do not come here'?" Mom asked.

"A complex one. *Come* is just one word. *Do not come here* is four words. Sadie obeyed perfectly."

"That's not funny, Willie," Mom said. "Remember, you've got one hour."

"Since when am I an expert on manners?" I protested. "I still eat with my elbows on the table. And I bring up disgusting subjects during meals. Remember when I described that mutilated possum with maggots eating its guts. I said it right when you served us white macaroni. Talk about bad timing. Orville lost his appetite, and Amanda lost more than that."

"Don't give me your excuses. Go get Sadie and start working with her," Mom ordered. "Now move it!"

I was about to make another excuse, but from the tone of my mom's voice, I knew I'd better keep quiet. As if Sadie's paws hadn't made things bad enough, my smart mouth had made things worse. "Sorry, Mom," I said, feeling guilty for being so disrespectful. "And this time I mean it."

I found Sadie hiding under my bed, licking the casserole from her paws. I dragged her downstairs and out the back door. Sam joined us outside and we got to work.

"Sadie, come!" I said.

Sadie pranced around as if I were talking to the moon.

"Maybe Sadie needs some motivation," Sam said. "What gets her attention?"

"That's easy. Food." I ran inside and grabbed a handful of dog biscuits. Walking to the back fence, I held out one of the treats and tried the same command. "Sadie, come!"

Sadie ran straight toward me and sat down right in front of me. She looked up at me and wagged her tail.

"It works!" I said, giving her the treat. While Sadie gobbled it down, I walked to the patio. Holding up another biscuit, I repeated the command. "Sadie, come!"

Sadie came right over. I rewarded her with another biscuit.

"Mom, come out here quick!" I said.

"What now?" she moaned, as if expecting to see another rosebush demolished.

"Watch this," I said. I walked to the back fence and repeated the procedure with Sadie. "See, Mom. Next time Sadie gets out, just grab a dog biscuit and tell her to come. She'll be back in no time."

My mom didn't look as impressed as I thought she should, but at least she didn't look as upset. "Well, that's a start. But I wouldn't get too confident until you've actually tried it," she said.

"No problem," I said. "Let's go." I walked to the front gate with Sadie following behind.

"Get the long leash, first," Mom cautioned, "just in case Sadie's not as obedient as you think."

"Don't worry, Mom," I said. "Sadie has this down. She knows this command."

Sam and Mom joined me at the gate. As soon as I pulled it open, Sadie bolted between our legs for the front yard.

"Not a problem," I said with a shrug. Strolling into the front yard, I extended a dog biscuit, the biggest one I had. By now Sadie was halfway down the street and moving like a greyhound chasing a rabbit.

"Sadie," I shouted. "Come!"

Sadie continued down the street, full throttle. I wouldn't look at my mom, but I could feel her eyes scorching my red hair.

"Sadie!" I shouted again as loud as I could, "Come!"

My mom cleared her throat.

"I mean it this time, Sadie," I went on, trying a kinder, more conversational approach. "Turn around immediately and come here. Seriously. Don't think I'm being sarcastic because I'm not." I tossed the dog biscuit in the air, hoping she would catch the scent on the breeze.

Sure. That happened. Sadie disappeared around the corner, still moving like a runaway train.

"Okay, don't come here then!" I yelled after her. Then I turned to my mom and chuckled softly. "See. She obeyed me that time. It's just a matter of picking the right command—one that corresponds with Sadie's particular mental state at the time it's given."

Sam grinned, trying to help me out.

Mom just glared. "What did I say about a leash?"

"I really thought that ..."

"Obedience school!" Mom said, cutting me off. "And until then, that dog stays outside."

The Last Heiress

Sam and I took off running. I knew exactly where to try to find Sadie: Colonel Pike's. Sure enough, when we arrived at the Pike Estate, we found Sadie. This time, though, she wasn't down in the tunnel. Colonel Pike had tied her to the front porch.

"Sadie, what am I going to do with you?" I asked, trying to catch my breath. Sadie jumped up on me and licked my face.

"That dog of yours has sure taken an interest in my place," the Colonel said, coming out on to the porch. "Unless you sent her yourself just so you could get another Cactus Cooler."

"I wish that's all this was about," I said. "But if you knew how mad my mom is, you'd realize that no Cactus Cooler is worth that."

"Oh, I don't know," Sam said. "Your mom didn't seem that mad to me."

"That's because she's not mad at you. It's Sadie and I that are in deep trouble."

I explained to Colonel Pike what had happened and the looming threat of obedience school.

"There's nothing wrong with a dog that knows how to obey. Pistol Pete would tell you that. He taught Sandy to fetch a pistol for him, just in case he ever got pinned down by outlaws," Colonel Pike told us.

Sam patted Sadie on the head. "What do you think, Sadie? Would you do that for Willie?" Sadie wagged her tail and barked.

"I'd say that's a yes, don't you think so, Colonel Pike?" I asked. He was staring at Sadie, but his eyes were glossed over like he was somewhere else.

"Colonel?" I asked again.

"I'm sorry," he said. "Every time I look at your dog, I think I've seen her before. I just don't know where."

"Maybe you saw her in your roses," Sam suggested. "Sadie has a thing for roses. Just ask Willie's mom."

"No, I don't think that's it," Colonel Pike said. He lifted his cavalry hat and smoothed his hand over his white hair. "Something tells me I saw your dog in a picture." He stared at Sadie, deep in thought.

"Any ideas?" Sam asked me. I just shrugged.

"Wait a minute," Colonel Pike said. "I think I may know. You kids have a seat on this bench. I'll be right back."

Colonel Pike walked back into the house. We could hear him walk across the wood floor and open what sounded like a closet door. When Colonel Pike returned, he had an old photo album as thick as the Plummet Family Bible. The black cover looked like it would disintegrate in his hands. He sat down between me and Sam and opened the album.

"No offense, Colonel Pike, but these pictures are *way* before Sadie's time," I explained.

"You got that right," he replied. "This album has some of the first photos ever taken of Glenfield." He wasn't kidding. A musty smell lifted from the pages. The pictures were all black and white with a brownish tint.

"These are some of the first settlers to arrive in this area. There's Hank Wheeler, the first sheriff." Colonel Pike pointed to a man with beady eyes and a long mustache shaped like a bull's horns.

Colonel Pike turned the pages slowly, carefully searching each photo. He identified some of the people and places; others he ignored. "There's the Stockgrowers Stagecoach," he said. "That was robbed a few times." When he said that, he paused and searched across his property, as if the photo brought back a memory that he wanted to forget but couldn't.

I glanced at Sam, not sure what to do.

"Here it is!" Colonel Pike announced. He had flipped to the last page, revealing a picture of two men and a dog. One of the men had on a coat and tie. The other wore chaps and a red bandanna. From his belt hung two six-shooters. The belt itself was lined with extra bullets. But the dog between them explained the Colonel's reaction.

"It's Sadie," I said, surprised by the perfect resemblance. The dog in the picture had the same markings: white chest, black front paws and shoulders, droopy ears, one hanging lower than the other. The dog's tongue even fell from the side of its mouth at the same angle as Sadie's.

"That's amazing," Sam said.

"Any idea who these people are?" Colonel Pike asked. Sam and I just shook our heads.

"The man in the suit is J.D. Pike, my granddaddy," Colonel Pike explained. "The cowboy next to him is none other than Pistol Pete himself. And the dog beside Pete is Sandy, his loyal cocker spaniel."

I stared at the photo, then looked at Sadie. She wagged her tail. I thought about what had happened over the last few days: Sadie's determination to come here, the digging, finding the tunnel. She'd even rejected a dog biscuit to run straight here. The connection seemed obvious, but I had to ask. "So you think Sadie's related to Sandy, Pistol Pete's dog?"

"I don't see why not," Colonel Pike replied. "Especially when you compare their markings. Do you know anything about Sadie's background?"

I shrugged. "We bought her from Grange Kennels. Have you heard of them?"

"Sure have," Colonel Pike said. "The Granges are old friends. They've been around Glenfield as long as I have. Sadie's connection to Sandy is looking better all the time. Let me give them a call."

We waited on the porch while Colonel Pike phoned the kennel. When he came back, the Colonel was grinning ear to ear. "Willie, you have an official heir of Sandy, Pistol Pete's dog. Keith Grange dug through some old records and traced Sadie all the way back to Sandy. Seems Sandy had a couple litters before she disappeared. And what's more, you have her last known descendant. Her last one."

I rose to my feet in awe. "Why didn't Mr. Grange tell me that when I bought her?"

"That's what I asked him. He didn't think kids today cared much about history. It seems like if it doesn't come on a CD-ROM or if it ain't on TV, you kids don't give a hoot." I had to look away. Before I'd met Colonel Pike, that described me perfectly and, at times, it still did.

"Do you think Sadie's connection to Sandy is what draws her back?" Sam asked.

"Must be," Colonel Pike replied. "She senses that her roots are here."

"Maybe she senses more than that," I said. "Maybe there's something in those tunnels, like gold."

Colonel Pike jumped as though I had triggered a nerve. Then he looked away, as if determined to downplay my remark. "I doubt it, but you're welcome to take her back down there for another look. Just let me know so I can let you in through the cellar. I closed up the hole under the bush for fear that the wrong element might start snooping around down there."

When Colonel Pike mentioned the "wrong element," I immediately remembered Mr. Rennis, the transportation supervisor. Whatever he had in that envelope the other day was obviously bad news for the Colonel. But I didn't know how to bring it up.

Since it was getting late, I decided to head home for some of Mom's casserole with the special mineral enrichment courtesy of Sadie. Not that anyone could get too mad about that. After all, Sadie was the final heir to a legend.

Crusher's Footsie

The next morning I could hardly wait to get to school. My popularity was sure to skyrocket. As soon as the kids at Glenfield Middle School found out about Sadie, they'd hoist me on their shoulders and carry me down the hall.

At the breakfast table my dad cautioned me. "Be careful not to come off as conceited, Willie. No one likes that attitude, and you may even get yourself into trouble."

"Trouble? I live for trouble," I said, flipping my head in the air. "I'm practically a descendant of Pistol Pete himself."

Orville let out a laugh, and Amanda shook her head. Dad just rolled his eyes.

As soon as I stepped on campus, I spread the word about Sadie. The response was big. Really big. Lots of my friends had grown up hearing about Pistol Pete from their grandparents. The church workday last Saturday had added to his popularity. But the information about Sandy, Pete's loyal dog, was news. I became the living link to a part of Pete's life that the kids at school knew little about. They were hungry for information.

"What kind of dog was Sandy?" Mitch asked.

"Just like Sadie, I guess," I told him.

"What's *Sadie* like?" Mitch's twin sister, Megan, asked.

"Intelligent. Loyal. Brave. She's like a canine book of virtues. A lot like her owner, I guess. But hey, don't take my word for it. Come by my house after school. For a buck you can shake Sadie's paw."

"A buck? That's worth it," Mitch said.

"Listen, I'm not in it for the money," I said. "I just want people to experience a piece of history."

"Count me in," several students replied.

"You got it," I told them, ready to seize the moment. "Until then, I've got a few mementos, if you're interested." I opened my jacket to reveal my wares. "Clips of Sadie's hair: 50 cents; color photos: two bucks; used flea collar: three dollars; chew-toy with teeth marks: five even, which is a steal considering it's a one of a kind item."

Students gathered around, pushing money in my face in exchange for Sadie merchandise. They didn't lift me onto their shoulders, but only because they were too busy reaching for their wallets or running off to tell their friends. By the time the first bell rang, I was the most popular kid in school. Even my teachers wanted to hear about Sadie, the living legacy of Pistol Pete.

When the lunch bell rang, I couldn't wait to get to the cafeteria. I'd sit at the head of a long table with all eyes on me. Several students had already promised me cuts.

Sure enough, as soon as I grabbed my tray, I was waved to the front of the line. The lunchroom lady slopped down an extra helping of meat loaf. Mitch even paid for my food while I strutted to a table and waited for my public to join me. Instead of my public, I got Felix.

"Willie, bad news," he said. "This Sadie-the-heiress stuff may have gone a little too far."

"Too far?" I questioned. "What's that supposed to mean? It's all true and people are eating it up."

"Not everyone," Felix said. He glanced over his shoulder like a wanted man.

"What do you mean, *not everyone?*" I asked.

"Let's just say Leonard isn't taking your announcement too well."

"As in Leonard 'the Crusher' Grubb?" I cringed.

Felix nodded. "He's the only Leonard at our school."

"What's his problem?" I asked, getting bothered.

"It turns out he has a pet connected to Mark Twain."

"Mark Twain, the author? Pistol Pete could whip Mark Twain with one gun tied behind his back."

"That's what I told Crusher," Felix told me. "But it didn't go over too well, especially when I learned what kind of pet he was talking about."

"Go ahead," I said. "Give me the news."

"It's a rabbit. Crusher has a pedigreed rabbit named Footsie that is a direct descendant of Mark Twain's pet rabbit."

"Footsie? Crusher Grubb has a rabbit named Footsie?" I slapped my forehead. "That's hilarious."

"Tell me about it. I had to bite my cheeks so Leonard wouldn't see me laughing. So did everyone else. Talk about willpower. It was a sight to behold."

"What did he do?"

"He had a fit!" Felix said, his eyes wide. "He accused you of making the whole thing up. He said Sadie was a fake."

"A fake? No way! You didn't let him get away with it, did you?"

"Not on your life," Felix explained, making a fist. "I told Crusher to watch it or Sadie might come over and have his little rabbit Footsie for lunch. Of course, I said that on your behalf."

"Of course," I moaned, looking under the table for a place to hide. I was too late. Crusher Grubb entered the cafeteria and marched straight for me. I grabbed Felix's arm before he could get away. "Don't leave me now, I.V. Man. I may need your superhuman strength to crush the Crusher."

"Sorry, dude," Felix conceded. "Those iron plates wiped me out. I can barely lift my arms." He moved behind me as Crusher Grubb stepped up in front of me.

"What's up, Leonard?" I asked as though everything were okay between us.

"You tell me, Plummet," he demanded.

"Just got some good news, that's all," I explained, determined to keep everything under control.

"You mean good *lies*," Leonard snarled. "You expect us to believe your dog is the direct descendant of Pistol Pete's dog?"

"It's true. Just ask the guy at Grange Kennels," I replied. "Or check out the picture in Colonel Pike's photo album."

"Why should I waste my time checking out your story? The whole thing's a joke. If you want to brag about your mutt having a famous ancestor, you need documents like I have for mine."

"What pet is that, Grubb?" I asked.

"My rabbit, Footsie," Crusher announced. Muffled laughter could be heard.

I gritted my teeth, determined not to bust up, but my face betrayed me.

"Something funny about my rabbit, Footsie?" he grunted.

I sucked in my cheeks. I had to maintain control.

"Rabbit Footsie," Crusher repeated. He stepped forward until his breath singed the ends of my red hair. His hands looked capable of crunching a shot put into fine powder. "If I were you, I would come up with some other proof in a real hurry. Otherwise that mutt of yours is going to be looking for a new master. You'll be history, Plummet, just like that outlaw Pistol Pete."

Felix and Sam shook their heads at me, as if anticipating what I was about to say. But I couldn't let Crusher push me around. I owned the sole descendant to Pistol Pete's dog, Sandy. If Pete always stood his ground, why shouldn't I?

"All right," I said. "You want proof? How about a secret tunnel? As in the one dug by Pistol Pete himself. Sadie found it the other day."

"Your dog found Pistol Pete's lost tunnel?" Crusher asked, disbelief heavy in his voice.

Sam and Felix swiped their fingers across their throats, trying to make me stop, but I wouldn't. "That's right. Sadie found it by instinct because it's in her blood."

"Where's the tunnel?" Crusher asked. "Huh?" This time Felix and Sam shook their heads even more vigorously. But reading the fire in Crusher's eyes, I knew I could either tell him or join Pistol Pete in history. *Way to go, Willie*, I told myself. You got conceited and look where it got you. Once again, Dad was right.

9

Felix Gets Fried

If it hadn't been for Mrs. Keefer, my English teacher, I would never have escaped the cafeteria alive. But just as Crusher was about to squeeze the tunnel's location out of me, she came over and broke things up. With a little more evasive action on my part, I was able to get through the rest of the day unscathed.

Felix left a note in my locker that asked me to meet him in the lab after school. I was only too happy to do it. Anything to avoid Crusher Grubb. Getting teased over his rabbit, Footsie, had really chapped his hide. The snickering behind his back didn't help either. Crusher Grubb wasn't used to being laughed at.

When I arrived at the lab, Felix looked pensive. "It's about time you got here," he told me.

"Sorry. I would have been here sooner, but I had to train Sadie," I explained. "Once people saw her, they kept stopping us."

"That's what you get for blabbing about the tunnel. They think if they're nice to you, you'll lead them right to it."

"Don't worry. That's not going to happen. I learned my lesson. Right, Sadie?" She wagged her tail in response. When I unhooked her leash, she found a cool spot next to the wall and lay down.

"Well, I think it's about ready," Felix said.

Three power boxes, like the kind from an electric train set, covered the operating table in the center of the lab. A dozen wires, each with a clamp on the end, led from the boxes.

"What are those for?" I asked.

"Before I answer that, I want you to know I'm sorry I didn't stand up for you today against Crusher Grubb," Felix said. "Next time I will, guaranteed."

"Oh you will, huh?"

"Absolutely. And here's why." Felix waved his hands across the power boxes on the table. "Say hello to EMS therapy, the scientific way to build muscle."

"What happened to *I.V. Man?*"

"Kid stuff. This is the wave of the future." Felix grabbed the clamps and fastened them to his arms, chest, and stomach. "EMS stands for electronic muscle stimulation. When you flip the power switch to "on," the electronic impulse contracts and relaxes each muscle group up to 70 times per minute. That's 70 sit-ups and 70 biceps curls and so on. Can you believe it? I'll look like Mr. Universe by the end of the week."

"Felix, no offense," I said, "but this seems like something I would try. You're the brains of the lab triangle. Why are you doing this?"

"You know why. I'm tired of being thin and known only for my brain. Besides, I did my research. This is a legitimate form of muscle development. The Russians have used EMS for years. It has even been approved by the Olympic committee. Now hurry up, these clamps are starting to hurt."

"You want me to shock you with enough voltage to light Disneyland and you're complaining about some skin clamps?"

"That's the beauty of EMS—it doesn't hurt. It's all a matter of gradual implementation. Now go ahead and trip the lever and watch my muscles expand before your eyes."

The three power boxes led to one control box. It had a lever and a meter next to it, which I guessed would rate the amount of muscle growth. "Are you sure you want me to turn this thing on?" I asked Felix. "These controls seem sort of complicated to me. I'm not sure …"

"There's no need for me to explain the technical details that you wouldn't understand anyway. Just hit the "on" switch," Felix told me. "The anticipation is killing me."

"What do you think the voltage will do?"

Felix closed his eyes and clenched his fists. "I'm ready when you are."

"Suit yourself." I slid the lever to the right, bracing myself for a shower of sparks. Nothing happened.

"Hurry up!" Felix said. "These clamps are brutal."

"I must have hit the wrong button," I said.

"Wait a minute. What button did you—"

"Here it is." I flipped the power switch to "on."

ZAP!

"Ahhhh!" Felix wailed. His face lit up like a 100-watt lightbulb. His eyes popped out of his head. His hair shot out from his head like optic fibers.

"W-W-Willie! T-T-Turn it off! N-N-Now!" Felix stuttered.

I hit the "off" switch as quick as I could. Felix continued to vibrate ... and smolder.

"Whoa! That was cool!" I said. "You look bigger already. Well, at least your hair does. A few more jolts like that and you'll be one massive muscle. Instead of *I.V.* Man, we'll call you *E.B.* Man for Electric Bulk."

I couldn't tell if Felix was shaking his head no or still twitching from the serious voltage that had rocked his body.

"Time to psych up for set number 2, Felix," I stated, accepting my role as his personal trainer. "Just tell me when."

With a trembling hand, Felix grabbed my throat. "W-W-What switch did you hit?"

"The power switch," I answered.

"Before that?"

"The one next to the meter. Why?" I asked.

"That's the voltage meter, you spaz. You turned the thing to max. That was like dropping a 500-pound barbell on my chest."

"I think it was you who said 'No pain. No gain'?" I reminded him. "Do you want to bulk up or not?"

"Not," Felix blurted out. "I want to live."

"That's fine with me. I've been in agreement with Colonel Pike all along. You look fine like you are. Now what do you say we head over to the tunnel for a little exploration. If we hurry, we can use your body as a human glowworm. Then you can be *I.T.* Man, for Illuminates Tunnel."

"No more, Willie," Felix begged. "Please, no more."

Java the Mutt

Getting to Colonel Pike's house without being followed was no easy feat. Between Sadie the celebrity and optic-fiber Felix, everyone in town noticed us. We finally had to duck into alleys and crawl under bushes until we made it to Colonel Pike's backyard. That's when he saw us and quickly brought us inside.

"Seems someone's been doing a little talking," he said, giving me a disappointed look.

"I'm sorry, Colonel. I was showing off. But I promise I didn't tell them *where* Sadie found the tunnel."

"I know. If you did, my yard would have been full of people by now." He bent down and patted Sadie. "How's the heiress doing today?"

"She's ready to dig," I said.

"And what about you, young man?" Colonel Pike asked Felix. "You look like you stuck your finger in a light socket. Not another muscle trick, I hope. I told

you, you look just fine the way you are. God knew what He was doing when He made you."

"What can I say?" Felix said with a shrug.

We followed Colonel Pike down to the cellar. He pulled back the buffalo hide and pushed open the beam door. After turning on our flashlights, the three of us followed Sadie into the tunnel.

"If I were you, I'd unhook Sadie's leash to see where she goes first," Colonel Pike suggested.

"Sounds good," I said, turning her loose.

Sadie trotted down the tunnel in no particular hurry. She sniffed the beams and scratched at the wall in some places. Colonel Pike shined the light on everything she touched, as if looking for a clue.

After walking a ways, Sadie stopped suddenly and began to dig in the wall.

"Maybe she's found something," I said. "Get it, Sadie." She scratched away at the dirt, pushing it between her back legs. Soon her entire body was inside the dirt wall.

"Man, she makes a lot of noise when she digs," Felix observed.

"You think that's loud, you should hear my mom when Sadie digs up her roses," I said. With my flashlight shining into Sadie's little tunnel, I monitored her progress.

Colonel Pike looked around. "I'm afraid that noise isn't just Sadie. Someone else is digging nearby, and whoever it is is getting closer." We shined our flashlights up and down the tunnel and along the ceiling, trying to figure out where the digging was coming from.

Then Colonel Pike moved down the tunnel to the spot where I had first fallen in a few days ago. "Well, Willie," he said, "it looks like your friends found your entrance. I guess my cover-up job wasn't good enough after all."

We watched the area where Sadie had first discovered Pistol Pete's tunnel. The dirt and gravel that Colonel Pike had used to plug the hole began to give way.

"Please, Lord," I whispered, "let it be anyone but Crusher Grubb."

As the mystery digger got closer, more and more dirt fell into the tunnel. We shined our lights on the spot, ready for a hand or a shovel to appear. What we saw was a paw—a big paw. The paw was followed by a long black nose and a set of sharp white fangs.

"Grrr!" the animal growled. It pushed through the rest of the dirt and dropped into the tunnel.

"It's a giant!" Felix squawked.

"It's a savage dog!" Colonel Pike added.

"It's Java," I said with a laugh. "Here, boy."

Java wagged his tail and came over to me. "Woof! Woof!" he barked.

"Easy big fella," I said.

His loud barking echoed inside the tunnel and sounded like thunder in our ears. Sadie quit digging and joined Java for some play. They wrestled and chased around like best friends. My efforts to get Sadie back to work were useless.

"There goes our treasure hunt," Felix complained.

"You got that right," Colonel Pike agreed. He stared at the hole in the wall that Sadie had dug. He was deep in thought.

"What is it?" I asked.

"Oh, nothing," he said. He lifted his hat and brushed back his white hair. "Why don't we call it quits for now? If you boys can take care of the dogs, I'll patch up that hole again. We can try searching some other day."

"Fair enough," I said, wishing we could stay. But with Java around, Sadie was uninterested in digging. As we headed for the cellar, Colonel Pike brought up the rear, sneaking a last glance at Sadie's new find. It was as if she had shown him the spot for something he had wanted to find for a long, long time.

Finding Java's house was easy because I had been there the other day. Last time, though, no one had been home. I hoped this time someone would be around. I knew Java's owner would want to know about his ability to get loose.

With a tight grip on Sadie's leash, I rang the doorbell and waited. Felix held on to Java's collar for all he was worth. Java stood higher than Felix's waist and probably could have dragged him down the street if he wanted to.

"Sit, Java," Felix commanded, trying to move away from Java's tail. "Ouch! That thing feels like a bullwhip." I rang the bell again. Still no response. I tried knocking but to no avail.

"I guess we'll just have to put him around back," Felix said.

We walked through the side gate and led Java into the backyard. That's when we heard a man's voice coming from inside the house. It was a one-sided conversation with pauses. He had to be on the phone. I wouldn't have thought much about it until he mentioned Colonel Pike.

"Rumor has it that some kids found the tunnel," the man grumbled. After a pause, he continued. "We can't risk them finding anything else. Get over there with your equipment and give them a scare." Another pause. "Just do it!" the man shouted, getting mad. "Only two more days and we can begin. Then we'll have all the access we need. If there's any gold down there, we'll find it."

The man slammed down the receiver. His heavy boots clomped across the floor.

"Hurry," I whispered to Felix.

Felix followed me back through the side gate to the front, making sure not to let Java loose. Once again I rang the doorbell.

The boots clomped to the other side of the front door and stopped. I swallowed hard and watched the door, not sure I wanted to know who lived inside. When the door swung open, I knew I didn't want to know. It was Mr. Rennis, the transportation supervisor.

The Real Story of Pistol Pete

After Felix and I returned Java, we headed back to Colonel Pike's as quickly as our knees would carry us. I say knees because we had to crawl under bushes and creep behind trees to avoid being seen. Two trips to the Pike Estate in one day would make anyone suspicious. Felix's muscle spasms didn't help either. He kept stopping, unable to control his legs and arms. And it didn't help that Sadie was fighting her short leash.

"Would you hurry up," I told Felix.

"If you hadn't turned my EMS device into the electric chair, I'd be fine," he reminded me.

"I told you to explain it to me," I said.

I had Felix lead the way. He served as a human lantern in the twilight, thanks to the ample wattage still flowing through his hair.

When we finally made it to the Pike Estate, I pounded on the front door, desperate to tell the

Colonel what we had learned. But he didn't answer. We pounded again and still no response.

"Maybe he's patching up the hole that leads to the tunnel," Felix suggested. "He said he would take care of it."

"Can't hurt to look," I replied. We crossed the backyard and ducked under the bottlebrush plant. Sure enough, the hole had been sealed over. But that didn't stop Sadie. She jerked to the end of her leash and immediately began to claw at the loose dirt like a T-bone steak was buried just below the surface.

"Sadie, no!" I ordered as I pulled her toward me. It didn't help. She fought to get back to the hole.

"Woof! Woof!" she barked, determined to keep digging.

"What's going on down there?" Felix asked. "Sadie's freaking out."

"Beats me," I said. Running to the back door, I knocked as loudly as I could. "If Colonel Pike gets mad, I'll be the first to apologize, but I think we should check the tunnel, just in case he's down there and something went wrong."

When Felix agreed, I tried the back door. It was unlocked. "Colonel Pike?" I yelled, stepping inside the house. "Colonel Pike?"

When he still didn't answer, we cut through the kitchen and made our way downstairs to the cellar. I pulled my flashlight from my pocket as Felix pulled aside the buffalo hide and pushed aside the beam.

Sadie got one look at the tunnel and lunged inside, jerking the leash from my hand.

"Sadie! Come back!" I shouted.

"Colonel Pike?" Felix yelled.

We worked our way through the tunnel after Sadie. She was returning to the hole she had dug earlier. When we caught up with her, she was scraping at the edge of a much bigger hole. A closer look revealed why. Colonel Pike's boots extended from the site of Sadie's excavation in the wall. He had been digging in the same spot.

"Colonel Pike?" we yelled, running toward him.

Sadie barked and tugged at his pant leg. The Colonel didn't budge.

Felix and I grabbed the Colonel's boots, ready to drag him out. We feared the hole had collapsed on his head and suffocated him.

As we started to pull, a low rumbling sound, like logs being sawed, relieved our fears. Colonel Pike was snoring.

"What's going on out there?" he stammered, kicking us away.

"It's Willie and Felix. Are you okay?" I asked.

"You betcha. I must have dozed off." Colonel Pike slid into the main tunnel and stood up. He used his cowboy hat to brush the dirt from his shirt and jeans. "I thought you boys went home."

"So did we," I explained. "But that was before we stopped by Java's house. You'll never guess who owns him."

"You're probably right," Colonel Pike admitted. "Who?"

"Mr. Rennis," I told him. "And what's worse, he's planning to get control of your tunnels."

Lines of anger creased Colonel Pike's forehead as I explained everything we had heard. I expected the Colonel to start shouting or to stomp up and down, he looked so mad. But when I finished, he just removed his red bandanna and wiped his face.

I remembered his sad expression the other day and wondered if a piece of his past, hidden long ago, had come to the surface. Turning toward the cellar, the Colonel asked us to follow him. Sadie followed without a fuss. Even she no longer cared about the hole she had started.

The Colonel had us wait in the cellar while he fetched a round of Cactus Coolers and his old photo album. Sitting down on an old cowhide sofa between me and Felix, the Colonel opened to a black-and-white picture of a woman wearing a big feather hat and a white blouse with long sleeves. Her black skirt went to the ground. If anyone looked like a pioneer, she did.

"Boys, that there is Emma Pike, my grandma. In the early 1870s she traveled from the East Coast to join my granddaddy, J.D. Pike, here in Glenfield. They

already were married, but he had come out ahead of
her to work as a circuit judge and find a place to settle. He purchased this place from Pistol Pete. Because
of all the things Pete did to help the law, he and my
granddaddy were good friends.

"Once he had purchased the property, J.D. went
to work on a big house, the one you are sitting in.
When it was nearly done, he sent for Grandma Emma
to join him. She was to travel west in an armored
stagecoach, complete with a cavalry escort, and bring
the family fortune with her. By the time she was to
arrive, the ranch house would be finished, thanks in
part to Pistol Pete. Of course Sandy was around too.
In fact, she helped dig the foundation.

"But on the day the stagecoach was to arrive, a
lone soldier stumbled into town. He said the stage
and soldiers had been ambushed by the Crawly Gang.
They had shot it up pretty good. The survivors were
pinned down where the stage had crashed next to
some big boulders. Emma and her son, Matthew,
were still alive, along with the stagecoach driver and
the marshal. That's it.

"Pistol Pete and J.D. didn't hesitate. They grabbed
their guns and saddled up their horses, determined to
rescue Emma and Matthew or die trying.

"When J.D. and Pete arrived, they could see
things looked bad. The stagecoach driver had died
and the marshal was shot up pretty good. Crawly had

at least 20 men. Somehow Pete and J.D. broke through to the pinned-down survivors.

"J.D. knew he had to get Emma and Matthew out of there. With bullets ricocheting all around, he lifted his wife and son onto a horse. Pistol Pete stood up with a six-shooter in each hand and fired at anything that moved. He hit a few of Crawly's men and sent the rest diving for cover. If you ask me, Pistol Pete was the best shot there ever was. He never got the acclaim that Wild Bill and Doc Holiday got, but he was a sight to behold just the same."

"What happened to J.D. and his family?" Felix asked.

"With Pete covering them, they got away. They rode straight to Glenfield. At that time, though, Glenfield had fewer people in it than the Crawly Gang. And half of the folks here were women and children. J.D. led everyone to Fort Harber for refuge. There he could get reinforcements and ride back to save Pete."

"Did he make it?" I asked.

Colonel Pike sighed. "The cavalry was slow to respond, so J.D. took off with the understanding that they would follow. When he rode by this house en route to the stagecoach, he realized that he needn't go any farther. Crawly and his men had fallen around the house, all caught on the wrong end of a Colt 45. It wasn't until J.D. stepped onto the porch that he saw Pistol Pete. He was propped up on a bench, his head leaning back against the wood siding. He held one hand over his ribs, but he couldn't keep the blood from seeping past his fingers.

"J.D. gave Pete some water, but it was too late. In a rasping voice, Pistol Pete asked about Emma and Matthew. 'They're fine,' J.D. told him.

"Then Pete motioned for J.D. to lean closer. Pete's hair was dark with sweat. Just breathing made him wince. 'I brought the strongbox,' he whispered. 'Crawly and his men came for it, but I held them off.' Pete closed his eyes for the last time. 'It's with Sandy. She's guarding it. Without her, I never ...'

"Pete didn't have the strength to finish. He went to stand before the Lord, like we all will one day. J.D. checked the tunnel right off, guessing that's what Pete meant, but he couldn't find Sandy or the strongbox full of gold."

"Did the cavalry ever show up?" I asked.

"Yep. And J.D. told them what Pete had said about his gold being with Sandy. Of course he didn't mention the tunnel. That was a secret and J.D. wanted to keep it that way. Otherwise bandits would come snooping around, eager to dig up the gold."

"Pete was a hero. Why do people still say he was an outlaw?" Felix asked.

"Some said he hid the gold on purpose, hoping to keep it for himself. Others said he struck a deal with Crawly, then double-crossed him. How else could he have made it back to Glenfield alive?"

"It does seem sort of unbelievable," I agreed.

"Like I said," Colonel Pike continued, "Pistol Pete was the quickest draw there was. He could do it."

"So the strongbox full of gold is what Mr. Rennis is after," I observed. "But how'd he learn about the tunnel?"

"Well, you know how kids are. Sometimes they have trouble keeping secrets. My daddy might have mentioned it to a few of his friends when he was growing up. From there the legend of Pete's tunnel just got passed on."

"Your dad?" Felix asked.

"That's right," Colonel Pike explained. "Matthew, the 10-year-old boy that Pete saved, was my father. You should have heard him tell the story I just told you. He lived it!"

"Your version was good enough for me," I said, totally in awe.

"Even if Mr. Rennis does know about the tunnel," Felix went on, "I still don't get what he's up to. It's still your land."

"Which is why Rennis wants to make it his land. As the transportation supervisor for the county, he has a lot of power. Remember the envelope he gave me? The letter inside serves notice that the streets adjacent to my property will be widened. I've tried fighting it, but there's nothing I can do. Once the streets are widened, Rennis will have direct access to the tunnel."

"Is that why you want the historic landmark designation?" Felix questioned. "To protect the property?"

"You bet," Colonel Pike said. "And if any place deserves it, this house does."

"Will you know before Friday?" I asked.

"I hope so," Colonel Pike said. "I sure do hope so."

12

A Diesel Stampede

Getting through Wednesday's classes was next to impossible. The clock moved slower than it does on the last day of school. All I could think about was returning to Pistol Pete's lost tunnel with Sadie. If anyone could find Pete's dog, Sandy, and that strongbox, it would be her. Every time I thought about that strongbox, visions of gold filled my mind. Gold flakes for breakfast. Gold sandwiches for lunch …

Crusher Grubb brought me back to reality. He stalked me like a tiger, waiting for me to slip up so he could move in for the kill. The library, the cafeteria, in the hall between classes—he followed me everywhere. At one point it looked like Felix would intervene, but as soon as Crusher stared him down, he backed away.

"Where's the tunnel, Plummet?" Crusher demanded, grabbing my collar. "Tell me now or I'll take it out on you and your mutt after school."

Twisting free, I slipped into Mr. Keefer's science class. I was so shook up I sat in the front row. Talk about going from the frying pan into the fire. Mr. Keefer's experiments were even more life threatening than Crusher.

But like always, the Lord was looking out for me. I not only made it through class, I made it through the day. Even the showdown with Crusher was avoided when he had to stay after school for getting one too many tardies.

"Where's Felix?" I asked Sam as we walked home. "Doesn't he want to go with us?"

"He hurried home to finish something he was working on last night," she explained. "He told me he'd meet us at Colonel Pike's."

After picking up Sadie and our flashlights, Sam and I headed for the Pike Estate. Since everyone was keeping an eye out for me and Sadie, Sam, Sadie, and I took our usual route through the alleys, under cars, and behind bushes. Felix just walked straight there and got to the Colonel's before we did.

"Welcome back," Colonel Pike said, letting us in the back door. "How's Sadie and her posse?"

"Ready to find the strongbox," I replied. Colonel Pike led us down to the cellar, pushed aside the buffalo hide, crawled through the narrow beam door, and paused inside the tunnel.

I unhooked Sadie's leash, expecting her to return to the same spot in the wall as the other day and begin digging again. Instead, she sniffed it for a moment and walked away.

"So much for that," Colonel Pike said sadly.

"Come on, Sadie," I prodded her. "Find Sandy and the gold."

As Sadie pranced around, sniffing beams and scratching at the ground, I turned my attention to Felix.

"So tell me, Electromagnetic Man, what's your latest scheme? No offense, but you don't look any buffer."

"That's because I haven't tried it yet. It won't be ready until tomorrow."

"I can hardly wait," I said.

We followed Sadie to the end of the tunnel. She sniffed one of the beams, then scratched at the wall. A moment later she hit a stone slab and stopped.

"I didn't think she'd get too far down here," Colonel Pike said. "This end of the tunnel is solid rock. It's amazing that Pete bore into it as far as he did."

"But if the tunnel ends in solid rock, what good would it have done him?" Sam asked.

"He had escape routes going to the surface at different points. J.D. filled them in when he built the house so no one could find the tunnel. But Pistol Pete knew where they were. Granddad said Pete used them when the Crawly Gang surrounded the house. That's how he defeated 20 men single-handedly."

As Sadie sniffed along the tunnel, a low rumbling could be heard in the distance. We exchanged glances. Dirt sprinkled down from the ceiling. The rumbling intensified, like an avalanche of boulders rolling toward the Pike Estate. Sadie barked and tromped back and forth as if she had just seen a cat.

"What is that?" Felix yelled, covering his ears.

"Stampede!" Colonel Pike yelled. He ushered us away from the rock walls. As more dirt rained down, a brown fog enveloped the tunnel. We covered our mouths with our shirts. Suddenly the flashlights were less help than headlights in thick fog. We moved slowly, feeling our way through the dust cloud. The sound was deafening.

"Sadie?" I called out.

Her nose pressed against my leg and I attached the lease. "Get us out of here," I told her. She jerked me along with Sam, Felix, and Colonel Pike close behind. The dirt in the air grew thicker, and we all started to cough.

"Keep going," the Colonel shouted. "We'll make it!"

I wanted to cover my ears, but I kept my arm over my head for protection. Not that my arm would help much if one of the cross beams came down. The thick plank would drive me into the ground like a human stake.

"Are you sure it's a stampede?" I yelled. "It sounds like a tank invasion!" I thought of those World

War II movies of tanks and armored vehicles thundering across the land, destroying everything in their path. Another minute and Pete's tunnel would cave in. Then Sandy wouldn't be the only one to disappear down here. I squinted to protect my eyes. A heavy dust lined my tongue and throat.

"Hang on," I yelled, looking backward.

Bam! Something hard knocked me in the head. Normally I would have been ticked, but when I saw what it was, I wanted to kiss it. We had made it to the beam that served as the secret door. "Thank You, Lord," I said. Hunching down I squeezed through the narrow opening into the cellar. With the sound of roaring machinery all around, I half-expected the six-inch barrel of a tank to greet me.

Once everyone had squeezed through the beam-door, Colonel Pike rushed past us for the stairs. We followed, eager to see what was going on and what the Colonel would do about it.

It didn't take long to find out. One look outside and it was obvious. The streets that bordered the Pike Estate were filled with bulldozers, tractors, dump trucks, and every kind of heavy machinery imaginable. Standing on the edge of Colonel Pike's property was Mr. Rennis, holding a clipboard and barking orders at one of his workers. It was Jake, the foreman who had loaned us the jackhammer the other day.

With eyes full of fire, the Colonel pushed open the front door and marched right up to Mr. Rennis.

Glad I'm not Mr. Rennis, I thought. It looked like the Colonel would hog-tie Mr. Rennis with barbed wire. But that wasn't the case or even close. Whatever Mr. Rennis said shut the Colonel up in a hurry. After shaking his head in disgust and kicking the pavement with his pointed boots, the Colonel returned to the house.

"What's going on?" I asked.

"Road expansion," Colonel Pike said solemnly.

"But that's not until Friday," Felix replied. "What are they doing here now?"

"Setting up. Getting everything in place. As long as they stay in the street, there's nothing I can do about it."

"Does that mean we can't search the tunnel anymore?"

"I'm afraid we can't," Colonel Pike said.

"Then Rennis wins," Sam said. "He came to scare us off and it worked."

That struck a chord with the Colonel. "Tell you what, I'll have a look down there tonight after the dust has settled. If the beams are all in place and everything looks sturdy, we might make one final search, as long as that machinery ain't moving. But Rennis can't know about it, otherwise those bulldozers will be driving up and down the street for sure."

"You got it," I said.

We were about to sneak out the back door when Colonel Pike had us leave through the front door instead. He followed us to the porch and lectured us for Rennis' benefit. With our heads hung low, we plodded down the steps and off the grounds as if banished forever.

Out of the corner of my eye, I noticed Rennis watching us. His smile grew larger and larger with every step we took.

13

Bionic Bullfrogs

On Thursday the lab smelled more like a fresh bakery than the back room of Plummet's Hobbies. I was helping my dad with customers and had to keep explaining to them that, regardless of how it smelled, we did not have any bread for sale.

I wanted to see what Felix was up to and even sneak a taste for myself, but he wanted to surprise me with the finished product. When he finally waved me back to the lab, my mouth was watering.

"Muscle mania, here we come," Felix announced. He lifted a large glass filled with runny oatmeal. At least that's what it looked like.

"Where's the fresh bread?" I asked, searching around. "The stuff you're holding looks disgusting."

"It's not about taste, Willie," Felix explained. "It's about results. This special formula will turn me into one big muscle."

"Oh, that sounds attractive," I said. "Count me in."

"Don't worry, I did." Felix lifted a second glass of brown swill from the operating table. "This is for you."

I swallowed hard, realizing my wisecrack had just backfired. "What's in that stuff—gutter water?"

"Not hardly. This is an advanced *and* concentrated protein powder. I call it Muscle Maker 2000. It's made of amino acids, growth-enhancing nutrients, and dry yeast. The yeast accounts for the fresh bread aroma."

"Yeast?" I gagged. "You can't be serious."

"Think about it, Willie. What happens to yeast when it comes in contact with warm liquids? It rises. A piece of dough expands to two or three times its original size."

"Big deal," I said, disappointed that there would be no fresh bread. "Eating a loaf of bread doesn't inflate muscles."

"No, but my formula will. First, the quick-digesting amino acids will travel to the independent muscle groups throughout the body. Second, the slow-acting yeast will begin to rise. Within six hours my muscles will double or even triple in size. To the average layperson, I'll look buffer than Arnold Schwarzenegger."

"More like puffier than the Pillsbury Doughboy. You'll have to wear your Iron Velcro suit just to keep from floating away."

Felix shook his head, determined to believe in his formula. "This is the real thing, Willie. Are you with me or not?"

I wanted to say "or not," but I knew how much Felix needed my support. Walking to the table, I picked up my glass. "To muscledom," I toasted.

"To muscledom," Felix agreed. We downed our glasses in one swig, then stared at each other as if our muscles would grow before our eyes.

Ten minutes later we were still staring. Something was definitely going on in my gut, I just didn't know *what*. Then the phone rang.

"Willie, it's for you," Dad hollered from the front of the store. "It's Colonel Pike."

I walked to the cash register and took the receiver from my dad. "Hi, Colonel, what's the update?"

"They haven't moved the machinery all day," he said. "I've checked the tunnel twice now, and it seems fine. If you want to bring Sadie by for another look, that's fine with me. Just don't let Rennis see you."

After sneaking to Colonel Pike's all week I knew that wouldn't be a problem, providing Sadie didn't bark and Muscle Maker 2000 didn't explode our bodies like grenades.

Felix and I picked up Sadie and went to Sam's to see if she was ready to go. Not only had she finished her chores, but she had her flashlight in hand. "I thought you'd never get here," she told us.

Ten minutes later we were in the alley behind the Pike Estate. Since the house sat on a corner lot, Rennis was able to park equipment in the front and on the side of the house. From his position atop one of the bulldozers, he could see the backyard perfectly.

"So much for our normal route to the back door," I said. "Maybe the side door will work." We hunched our way to the street and crouched behind a steamroller.

"It's do-able," Sam said. "If we can crawl under the dump truck without being seen, there's just a quick dash to the house. Let's just hope the side door is unlocked."

"I'm not sure I can do anything quick," Felix stated. He loosened his belt a notch. "I don't feel so good."

"You don't look so good," Sam told him. "No offense, Felix, but you look more like a pear than a person. What'd you have for lunch, a balloon burger?

Sam was right. Felix did look sort of inflated. But then again, I didn't feel so hot either.

"Felix, are you sure that was slow-acting yeast?" I asked, rubbing my stomach. My skin felt tight, like an inner tube.

"That's what my mom said," Felix explained. "Then again, I never was much of a cook. My specialty is science." If I'd had a needle, I would have popped Felix then and there, but before I could do anything, Sadie let out a bark.

"Quiet!" I ordered, clenching my teeth.

"Woof! Woof!" she barked. I yanked the leash, desperate to calm Sadie down. But she didn't stop barking. A moment later I knew why. Java had arrived on the scene.

The two of them jumped around like the happiest dogs in the world. That I could handle, but the yapping had to stop.

"Quiet," I ordered again. I closed Sadie's mouth with my hand. When Sam tried the same with Java, he just jumped away and wagged his tail, like it was all a big game.

"Shhh!" Sam hissed, squinting hard at Java. He finally calmed down.

I looked around the steamroller to check on Rennis. He had climbed down from the bulldozer to talk with Jake.

"Now's our chance," I said. But even as I said it, I had my doubts. It felt like someone had taken an air hose to my gut. I looked down to loosen my belt, but I couldn't find it. My belly had swallowed it whole.

"What did you guys eat, anyway?" Sam asked. Felix explained Muscle Maker 2000 to her.

Sam just shook her head. "I can't believe you thought that would work! Felix, you're a genius, but lately you've been doing some pretty dumb things."

"It's this muscle thing," Felix confessed. "I'm sick of being thin. I'll try anything to put on some size."

"Oh, you're putting on size all right," Sam acknowledged. "If we wait a few more minutes, you can float to the Colonel's."

"This was your idea, Felix. What do you think we should do?" I demanded, trying to lower my voice.

Felix started to speak but quickly shut his mouth. His eyes filled with panic.

"What is it? Tell me," I muttered, getting mad. "What's your idea?"

Felix shook his head. He clamped his lips and covered them with his hand.

"Come on," I persisted. "Out with it!" I pulled his hand away from his mouth. Not a smart move.

"BURPPP!" Felix belched. My red hair whipped back like I was standing in a wind tunnel.

"Yuck," I gagged. "That was sick. That was— BURPPPP!"

Sam covered her ears. Sadie pulled her tail between her legs. Java ran away.

"BURP!" Felix sounded off.

"BURP!" I replied.

We sounded like bionic bullfrogs, but at least we felt better.

"Do you think they heard us?" I asked.

"They heard you in Hawaii," Sam said.

She was probably right, but I had to find out for sure. I peaked around the steamroller. Rennis stared back at me with a cruel grin on his face. A moment later he ordered Jake to climb on the bulldozer and turn the key. The diesel engine rumbled with hunger as it gobbled up the distance between us.

A New Way to Honor

"Let's go!" Felix yelled as he turned and ran back the way we had come. Well, running wasn't exactly the right word for it—maybe rolling was better. Of course, I didn't move much faster.

Sam and I followed Felix. Sadie was as eager to get away from the loud machinery as I was. I knew Rennis was laughing at us as we ran away.

Sam and I finally caught up to Felix a couple blocks later. After stopping to catch our breath (and let our stomachs settle down), we agreed to call it a night.

"I can't believe we couldn't make it to the house," I said. "We were so close."

"And now we've only got tomorrow afternoon to find Sandy and the gold," Sam added.

"I'll call Colonel Pike when I get home and tell him we'll be over after school tomorrow," I offered.

"I hope you guys won't be drinking any more of that disgusting concoction," Sam said. "It could be lethal in the tunnels."

"I can safely say that Muscle Maker 2000 won't be on my diet anymore," Felix said. He still looked like a balloon.

We agreed to meet at my house after school, then we went our separate ways.

I called Colonel Pike as soon as I got home. He agreed that the best plan was to put off our exploration until tomorrow.

I wasn't really hungry, but Mom insisted I eat dinner. I nibbled at my meat loaf, too full of Muscle Maker 2000 and disappointment to eat my normal three slices.

As if I weren't feeling discouraged enough, after dinner I decided to work with Sadie on her obedience problem. But she was so worked up from seeing Java, she was impossible to control.

"Come," I shouted.

Sadie took it to mean *don't* come. When I tried to catch her by the collar, she crouched low on her front paws with her rear end in the air. As soon as I got close, she sprang out of reach.

Playing fetch didn't go any better. I held a stick to her face, then tossed it across the yard. She just looked at me as if to ask, "What'd you do that for?" To show her I walked across the yard and picked up the stick. Then I realized the only one playing fetch was me. That's also when I noticed Sadie's recent paw prints around Mom's roses.

"Sadie!" I whispered furiously, careful not to alert my mom. The long-stem rosebushes had been uprooted and trampled into the mulch. I tried to replant them, but a thorn pierced my finger. "That's it," I said, accepting my defeat. "I quit."

Stomping to the back porch, I sat down and dropped my head between my knees. "Can things possibly get any worse?" I wondered out loud. We didn't just fail to find Sandy and the strongbox, thanks to Rennis we never even made it to the tunnel. The National Historic Landmark approval for the Pike Estate still hadn't arrived. Crusher Grubb wanted the tunnel's location or my hide, whichever came first. Felix had practically blown us to bits from the inside out with his lame Muscle Maker 2000 formula. Sadie wouldn't know a command if it yanked her by the leash. And once Mom found her rosebushes, I'd be sentenced to 10 weeks of obedience school.

As if sensing my thoughts, Sadie walked over and laid her head on my shoe. Her droopy eyes met mine.

"Sadie, what am I going to do with you?" I asked, giving her a pat. "You can't find Sandy or gold, but you're on Mom's roses like smoke on fire."

"Did I hear something about Mom's roses?" Dad asked, appearing at the back door.

"You don't want to know," I replied.

"Probably not, but you should probably tell me anyway." Dad sat down next to me. I filled him in on Sadie's most recent destruction job, along with everything else that was frustrating me.

"Dogs can be like that," he said. "I know. But they're still the best pet a kid could hope to have. They're loyal, protective, and always happy to be with you, like you're the most important person on earth." I looked at Sadie again. She lifted her head and wagged her tail.

"See what I mean?" Dad said. "You look at her and she's happy."

"Did you have a dog when you were growing up?" I asked.

"You bet. You won't believe it, but her name was Critter. She was a purebred Irish setter, a beautiful dog."

"Did she obey any better than Sadie does?"

"Not really, but I still loved her. In our house, no socks were safe on the floor. She'd carry them into the yard. When she got out front, I'd have to chase her all over the neighborhood. She wouldn't fetch a stick if it was wrapped in beef jerky. But I sure enjoyed having her around. I used to put on my dad's leather gloves and wrestle her to the ground. Then I'd run off and she'd chase me. One time my mom made a casserole with sardines. If it wasn't for Critter, I would have been a goner."

"Critter sounds like a cool dog," I said. "How come you never told me about her before?"

"You never asked," my dad said. "Plus it's hard to think about her without feeling a little sad. At 4 years old she got really sick and we had to put her to sleep. It was terrible." My dad's eyes were shiny when he finished. Reaching down to pet Sadie, he kept blinking.

Something my dad said stuck in my mind. "You never asked." He was right and I knew it. Somewhere along the line I had become convinced that my dad's stories were boring. Either that or they didn't relate. But I was wrong. It helped to hear about his dog, and it would help to hear about other things too. Like his best memory of junior high or his worst. His closest friends and where they hung out. There were so many things I didn't know about my dad simply because I never asked.

I knew I honored my dad when I obeyed him. But our youth pastor always said honoring meant a lot more than obeying. It meant loving your parents and respecting them. He'd reminded us how Jesus had made sure John would take care of Mary like his own mother. And Jesus did that while suffering all the pain of dying for us. Suddenly a new way of honoring Dad came to mind: I could show an interest in his life.

"Thanks for talking with me, Dad," I said, bumping his arm. "I feel a lot better."

"Anytime," he said. Before Dad went inside, he surveyed the damage to Mom's roses. "Willie, I know you're against obedience school, but try and be more open. The training would be good for Sadie and I know she'd appreciate the time with you."

At the sound of her name, Sadie lifted her head. Then she looked over at me as if waiting for my response.

The Secret Vault

We made it to Colonel Pike's as fast as we could on Friday. It was 3:20 P.M., which gave us less than an hour to find Sandy and the strongbox full of gold coins. At least this time Rennis didn't see us. Felix was through with his muscle-building schemes, which meant one less problem to overcome.

At the Pike Estate we expected to see lots of men around getting ready to dig up the yard for the road expansion. But Rennis and Jake, the foreman, were the only ones there. From the living room window we could see Rennis checking his watch constantly.

"We'd better get a move on," Colonel Pike instructed. Making our way to the cellar, we pushed aside the buffalo hide, moved the beam, and entered the tunnel.

"It's now or never, Sadie," I told her, shining my flashlight along the dirt floor. With her leash unhooked, Sadie pranced through the tunnel, wagging her tail.

The dark passageway, lined with beams and rock, had become a second home to her over the last week.

"You can do it, girl," Sam said. When Sadie stopped to sniff a beam, Sam gave her a pat.

Felix did too. "Come on, Sadie, find us the gold."

Colonel Pike brought up the rear, carrying a bright lantern. Sadie scratched at the wall in a few different spots, then let out a bark.

"What is it, girl?" I asked.

After a quick glance in my direction, Sadie picked up the pace. She went straight to the end of the tunnel.

"Here we are again. Nothing but solid rock," Colonel Pike lamented. "Oh well, I knew finding that strongbox was a long shot. If us Pikes haven't been able to locate the gold in more than 100 years, why would Sadie be able to do it in just one week?"

"Because Sadie is a sniffing, digging machine," I said, trying to keep my faith alive. "And not only that, she's the only remaining heir to Sandy. This tunnel is in her blood."

"No offense, partner, but right now the only thing in her blood is rock," Colonel Pike said.

Sadie sniffed at the rock enclosure. The massive slab didn't just mark the end of the tunnel, it formed the walls on both sides of us. No wonder Colonel Pike was discouraged.

I traced my flashlight along the two final support beams. The one on the left was actually embedded in the rock slab. At least that's how it looked at first. On closer examination I realized that the beam was wedged between the side rock and the end rock.

"It's a wonder Pistol Pete even bothered with that support beam," I observed. "He could have just rested the ceiling supports on the rock itself."

"Yep. It's hard to know what Pistol Pete had in mind," Colonel Pike said. He looked at his watch. "We're down to 15 minutes. We'd better call it quits. I wouldn't want to be down here when Rennis gets started."

Grabbing Sadie's leash, I gave her a jerk. As much as I wanted to keep looking, I knew that the Colonel was right. But Sadie wouldn't come. She sniffed at the wedged beam and let out a bark.

"Come on, Sadie," I said. "You gave it your best shot. Let's go."

"Woof! Woof!" she went on, scratching at the beam. Suddenly all our lights were fixed on the beam. Colonel Pike tried to look behind it but couldn't. The wood was wedged too snugly between the rocks.

"Colonel Pike," Felix asked, "does that beam look wider to you?"

Colonel Pike made a quick comparison with the other beams. "I think you're right." Sam went over and knocked on the beam, but it sounded as solid as the rock on both sides of it.

"You can't expect a block of wood that thick to sound hollow," I said. Sadie scratched at the bottom of the beam and barked some more.

"Wait a minute," I said. "Maybe it's just like the beam that leads to the cellar. Try pushing it in."

Sam kneeled down and put her shoulder to the wood. She pushed with all her strength, but the beam didn't budge. "Any more ideas?" she asked.

"How about if we all push?" Felix suggested. "If it hasn't moved in more than 100 years, it's bound to be stuck." We all gathered at the bottom of the beam.

"On three," Colonel Pike told us. "One. Two. Three!"

We heaved. We pushed. My feet started to slide out from under me, but I dug in and strained against the wood.

"Harder!" Colonel Pike commanded.

"Never surrender!" I added. We shoved with all our might.

"More!" Felix grunted.

"I'm all over it!" Sam shouted.

Then it happened. The beam moved! Just an inch, but it moved. Then it moved another inch.

"It's working!" Colonel Pike announced. We strained harder, pushing and shoving. The bottom of the beam gradually swung into the wall between the massive slabs.

"Just a little more," the Colonel said.

We heaved with what strength we had left, driving our shoulders into the splintery old lumber. As the top of the beam swung out, the bottom swung in. Soon it was possible to pass underneath it.

Colonel Pike held his lantern in a trembling hand, still stunned over what was happening. I felt the same way and could tell Felix and Sam did too.

Holding the lantern into the dark passageway behind the beam, Colonel Pike told us that he would go first. We kept our flashlights on him as he squeezed between the rocks. After going about six feet, he let out a yell. "Eureka!"

"What?" we asked. "What is it?"

"Come see for yourself," the Colonel replied.

With Sadie in front, I squeezed through the narrow stone passageway. Felix and Sam followed. We entered a natural cavern the size of a vault. The floor, ceiling, and walls were solid rock.

"This rules!" I said in awe. "Talk about the perfect hideout."

"Or tomb," Colonel Pike replied. He directed his flashlight to the back corner. Sandy's bones rested on top of a worn red blanket. When we gathered around, Colonel Pike pointed out a lead bullet still trapped in Sandy's rib cage. Sadie sniffed the bones for a moment, then laid down next to them and softly whined.

"Why would Pistol Pete shoot Sandy?" Felix asked.

"He didn't shoot her," Colonel Pike replied. "I'm sure of that."

I shined my flashlight around the room. "What do you think happened to the strongbox?"

"I have a hunch it's right here," Colonel Pike said. He carefully pulled aside the red blanket, making sure not to disturb Sandy's bones. The dirt beneath the blanket was loose.

Using his pocket knife, Colonel Pike began to dig. "I hit something!" he said.

We all scraped at the dirt. Soon the strongbox appeared. It was the size of a toolbox and had a handle on top. Colonel Pike pulled it to the surface.

A rolled up piece of brown paper was tied to the handle. Colonel Pike unrolled the paper so we all could read it.

Dear J.D., Emma, and Matthew,

Ran out of bullets when you left. My foot was shot up pretty good. Crawly Gang had me pinned between some rocks. Had to hold them off or they'd come for you.

The marshal was dead, but Sandy was still with me. Sent her for a box of ammo near the stagecoach. She made it but got hit on the way back. I pulled her to cover. Loaded guns and opened fire. Crawly and his gang ducked for cover. I rode here with the strongbox and Sandy. She died on the way.

Sandy deserves a fitting burial, with a tombstone and all, but Crawly and his gang will come soon. I've got to make a last stand for the folks who died on that stage. And for Sandy.

If you found this note, you found Sandy. If you'd bury her for me, I'd be much obliged.

Pistol Pete
July 30, 1887

Colonel Pike rolled the note back up and rubbed his eyes. "Well, there you have it. It wasn't just Pistol Pete who saved my family, Sandy did too. And thanks to Sadie, she's finally going to get the burial she deserves. But first we ought to see what's in this old iron box."

We turned our attention to the strongbox. The oldest padlock I'd ever seen secured the clasp.

"That shouldn't be hard to break off," I said.

The Colonel reached into his pocket. "No need. Grandma Emma had the key with her on the day the stage was robbed. She passed it on to my daddy. He passed it on to me."

With the turn of the key, the lock came loose. We shined our flashlights on the strongbox as Colonel Pike opened the lid. A pile of gold coins glimmered in the light. We dropped our mouths in awe at one of the most incredible sights we had ever seen.

"Well, I'll be!" Colonel Pike exclaimed.

"You're rich!" I gasped.

"And then some," Felix added.

"And just in time," Sam reminded us, looking at her watch. "It's four o'clock. We'd better get out of here." She helped Felix fold up the blanket with Sandy's bones.

Colonel Pike locked the strongbox. Suddenly a heavy rumbling shook the cavern.

"Too late," I shouted, covering my head. It sounded like a fleet of 18-wheelers had converged above us.

The walls shook; the ground quaked. It felt like we were in a giant trash compactor.

"Get a move on!" Colonel Pike ordered. Sam kneeled down to squeeze through the passageway, but she didn't fit! The walls had moved together. I led Sadie to the opening, but her shoulders were too wide.

Felix pushed past us. "Let me try." He turned sideways and exhaled. He squirmed into the narrow opening. I pushed his feet. He made it!

"It's only tight at the mouth of the cavern," he said over his shoulder. "The rest of the passageway is fine. Try chipping away at the rock while I go for help." I watched Felix disappear into the main tunnel.

"Like I said, God made him that way for a reason," Colonel Pike told us. He tried chipping away at the rock with the strongbox, but it didn't work. "What we need is a jackhammer."

"Or a helmet," I said, ducking. Bits of rock continued to fall from the ceiling. We covered our heads, praying that Felix could get them to shut down the machinery before it was too late. The walls trembled. Dust filled the air, making it hard to breathe. Sadie barked and I coughed.

"Maybe this will work," the Colonel said. He removed the padlock and swung at the closed-off opening, determined to chip loose enough rock to let us squeeze by. But he didn't need to. Just as quickly as the machines had started, they stopped.

"Felix did it!" I shouted. "He got to Rennis in time!" Sam and I gave the Colonel a hug. Sadie licked our faces and we fell over laughing.

Soon we could hear footsteps in the tunnel, followed by Felix's voice. "We're coming, guys. Hang on."

We focused our flashlights on the cavern opening. Seconds later Felix's squinting eyes appeared. "Mr. Rennis is with me to help. Jake took off to find the jackhammer. He'll be here soon."

"Slide on in there so I can see the situation," Mr. Rennis said. "Maybe a jackhammer's not enough."

Felix squeezed back into the cavern with us and Mr. Rennis' face appeared in the opening. He used my flashlight to examine the mouth of the cavern where the rocks squeezed together. "You were right," he said to Felix. "A jackhammer should break this up. The rest of the passageway is fine."

"Then what are you waiting for?" the Colonel asked, still mad at Rennis for all the trouble he had caused.

Rennis shined my flashlight on the Colonel, then on the box he was holding. "What do you have there, Colonel?"

"Something that's been in the family for a long time," Colonel Pike replied. "That's all I'm saying."

"I'm afraid that's not enough," Rennis told him. "Now hand it over." He produced a gun and pointed it at the Colonel.

We all froze, too stunned to say anything. My heart went into overdrive.

"Rennis, you're making a big mistake," Colonel Pike said.

"Oh, am I?" he scoffed. "If it took more than 100 years to find this tomb, how long will it take someone to find you? Now slide me the gold."

Colonel Pike looked at us, then slowly slid the strongbox to Rennis. As soon as Rennis saw the gold coins, his eyes glazed over. Grabbing a handful, he let the coins run through his fingers as if nothing else in the world mattered.

That's all Sadie needed. She lunged forward and bit the hand holding the gun.

"Yeow!" Rennis yelled, dropping the pistol to the ground.

With Sadie latched onto his hand, I kicked the gun out of the way. Then Colonel Pike picked up the iron strongbox and dropped it on Rennis's head, knocking him out cold. Sam scrambled to the gun, picked it up, and gave it to the Colonel.

After getting Sadie to let go of Rennis, I gave her a hug. "You're the hero today, Sadie. Sandy would be proud."

"Sadie's not the only hero," Colonel Pike reminded us. "If it hadn't been for Felix and his lean frame, we would all have been crushed to death."

"That's for sure," I said, giving him a pat on the back. "Good thing you didn't drink any Muscle Maker 2000 today."

We enjoyed a laugh while waiting for Jake to arrive with the jackhammer. Colonel Pike kept the gun at his side, just in case the foreman tried anything. But Jake was just as shocked as we were to learn about Rennis.

"I knew he wanted to search for the gold," Jake explained. "But I never thought it would come to this."

With Rennis still knocked out, Jake pulled him into the main tunnel. After just a few minutes of work with the jackhammer, the opening was large enough so we could get out.

Once we made it to the house Colonel Pike called the police. As Rennis was led to the police car, Colonel Pike turned his porch into a makeshift stage where he informed the growing crowd about Pistol

Pete's lost vault, Sandy's bravery, his grandparents' gold, and how Felix and Sadie had saved the day.

When Felix heard his name, he straightened his shoulders, looking more confident in his lean build than ever before.

"My only regret," the Colonel concluded, "is that much of this historical site will be destroyed because of the road expansion."

"Don't be so sure," a man said, stepping out of the crowd. He introduced himself as a federal employee. "I came here today to make a final inspection regarding an application we received. And I'm proud to say that your request has been approved."

The man turned to face us all. "Folks, I'd like to present to you the J.D. Pike Estate—Glenfield's first national historic landmark."

Everyone burst into cheers and applause. I ran over and gave the Colonel a high five. Sam and Felix did the same. Even Sadie jumped on the Colonel and barked with approval. That's when Java appeared and joined in the fun.

"What's going to happen to Java now?" I wondered out loud.

"He can stay here as long as he wants to," Colonel Pike offered. "But not without some obedience training. How about if you and Sadie join me and Java in that obedience class tomorrow?"

"Deal," I said.

"Good for you, Willie. That ought to make your mom a happy woman," Sam said.

"I hope so," I said, "but just in case, Sadie and I will pick her up a dozen roses on the way home."